HERE ARE LADIES

JAMES STEPHENS

1st WORLD
LIBRARY
Literary Society

Here are Ladies

James Stephens

© 1st World Library, 2006
PO Box 2211
Fairfield, IA 52556
www.1stworldlibrary.com
First Edition

LCCN: 2007920660

Softcover ISBN: 978-1-4218-3972-1
Hardcover ISBN: 978-1-4218-3872-4
eBook ISBN: 978-1-4218-4072-7

Purchase *"Here are Ladies"*
as a traditional bound book at:
www.1stWorldLibrary.com/purchase.asp?ISBN=978-1-4218-3972-1

1st World Library is a literary, educational organization
dedicated to:

- Creating a free internet library of downloadable ebooks

- Hosting writing competitions and offering book
  publishing scholarships.

Interested in more 1st World Library books?
contact: literacy@1stworldlibrary.com
Check us out at: www.1stworldlibrary.com

1st World Library Literary Society

Giving Back to the World

"If you want to work on the core problem, it's early school literacy."

- James Barksdale, former CEO of Netscape

"No skill is more crucial to the future of a child, or to a democratic and prosperous society, than literacy."

- Los Angeles Times

Literacy... means far more than learning how to read and write... The aim is to transmit... knowledge and promote social participation."

- UNESCO

"Literacy is not a luxury, it is a right and a responsibility. If our world is to meet the challenges of the twenty-first century we must harness the energy and creativity of all our citizens."

- President Bill Clinton

"Parents should be encouraged to read to their children, and teachers should be equipped with all available techniques for teaching literacy, so the varying needs and capacities of individual kids can be taken into account."

- Hugh Mackay

CONTENTS

WOMEN

Listen! If but women were
Half as kind as they are fair
There would be an end to all
Miseries that do appal.

Cloud and wind would fly together
In a dance of sunny weather,
And the happy trees would throw
Gifts to travellers below.

Then the lion, meek and mild,
With the lamb would, side by side,
Couch him friendly, and would be
Innocent of enmity.

Then the Frozen Pole would go,
Shaking off his fields of snow,
To a kinder clime and dance
Warmly with the girls of France.

These; if women only were
Half as kind as they are fair.

THREE HEAVY HUSBANDS

I

He had a high nose. He looked at one over the collar, so to speak. His regard was very assured, and his speech was that short bundle of monosyllables which the subaltern throws at the orderly. He had never been questioned, and, the precedent being absent, he had never questioned himself. Why should he? We live by question and answer, but we do not know the reply to anything until a puzzled comrade bothers us and initiates that divine curiosity which both humbles and uplifts us.

He wanted all things for himself. What he owned he wished to own completely. He would give anything away with the largest generosity, but he would share with no one—

"Whatever is mine," said he, "must be entirely mine. If it is alive I claim its duty to the last respiration of its breath, and if it is dead I cannot permit a mortgage on it. Have you a claim on anything belonging to me? then you may have it entirely, I must have all of it or none."

He was a stockbroker, and, by the methods peculiar to that mysterious profession, he had captured a sufficiency of money to enable him to regard the future with calmness and his fellow-creatures with condescension—perhaps the happiest state to which a certain humanity can attain.

So far matters were in order. There remained nothing to round his life into the complete, harmonious circle except a wife; but as a stated income has the choice of a large supply, he shortly discovered a lady whose qualifications were such as would ornament any, however exalted, position—She was sound in wind and limb. She spoke grammar with the utmost precision, and she could play the piano with such skill that it was difficult to explain why she played it badly.

This also was satisfactory, and if the world had been made of machinery he would have had the fee-simple of happiness. But to both happiness and misery there follows the inevitable second act, and beyond that, and to infinity, action and interaction, involution and evolution, forging change for ever. Thus he failed to take into consideration that the lady was alive, that she had a head on her shoulders which was native to her body, and that she could not be aggregated as chattel property for any longer period than she agreed to.

After their marriage he discovered that she had dislikes which did not always coincide with his, and appreciations which set his teeth on edge. A wife in the house is a critic on the hearth—this truth was daily and unpleasantly impressed upon him: but, of course, every man knows that every woman is a fool, and a tolerant smile is the only recognition we allow to their whims. God made them as they are—we grin, and bear it.

His wife found that the gospel of her husband was this—Love me to the exclusion of all human creatures. Believe in me even when I am in the wrong. Women should be seen and not heard. When you want excitement make a fuss of your husband.—But while he entirely forgot that his wife had been bought and paid for, she did not forget it: indeed, she could not help remembering it. A wrong had been done her not to be obscured even by economics, the great obscurer. She had been won and not wooed. (The very beasts have their privileges!) She had been defrauded of how many teasing and provoking prerogatives, aloofnesses, and surrenders, and her body, if not her mind, resented and remembered it.

There are times when calmness is not recognised as a virtue. Of course, he had wooed her in a way. He took her to the opera, he gave her jewels, he went to Church with her twice every Sunday, and once a month he knelt beside her in more profound reverences: sometimes he petted her, always he was polite—

But he had not told her that her eyes were the most wonderful and inspiring orbs into which a tired man could look. He never said that there would not be much to choose between good and evil if he lost her. He never said that one touch of her lips would electrify a paralytic into an acrobat. He never swore that he would commit suicide and dive to deep perdition if she threw him over—none of these things. It is possible that she did not wish him to say or do such extravagances, but he had not played the game, and, knowing that something was badly wrong, she nursed a grievance, that horrid fosterling. He was fiercely jealous, not of his love, but of his property, and while he was delighted to observe that other men approved of his taste, he could not bear that his wife should admire these outsiders. This was his attitude to her: Give me your admirations, all of them, every note of exclamation of which you are mistress, every jot and tittle of your thoughts must be mine, for, lacking these, I have nothing. I am good to you. I have interposed between you and the buffets of existence. I temper all winds to the bloom of your cheek. Do you your part, and so we will be happy.

There was a clerk in his office, a black-haired, slim, frowning young man, who could talk like a cascade for ten minutes and be silent for a month: he was a very angry young man, with many hatreds and many ambitions. His employer prized him as a reliable and capable worker, liked his manners, and paid him thirty-five shillings per week—Outside of these matters the young man abode no more in his remembrance than did the flower on the heath or the bird on the tree. It happened one day that the employer fell sick of influenza and was confined to his bed. This clerk, by order, waited on him to see to his correspondence; for, no matter who sneezes, work must be attended to.

The young man stayed in the house for a week, and during his sojourn there he met the lady. She fair, young, brooding! he also young, silent, and angry! After the first look had passed between them, there was little more to be said. They came together as though they had been magnetised. Love or passion, by whatever name it is called, was born abruptly. There is a force in human relations drawing too imperatively for denial; defying self-interest, and dragging at all anchors of duty and religion. Is it in man only the satisfaction of self? Egotism standing like a mountain, and demanding, "Give me yourself or I will kill myself." And women! is their love the degradation of self, the surrender and very abasement of lowliness? or is it also egotism set on a pinnacle, so careless and self-assured as to be fearful of nothing? In their eyes the third person, a shadow already, counted as less than a shadow. He was a name with no significance, a something without a locality. His certain and particular income per annum was a thing to laugh at . . . there was a hot, a swift voice speaking—"I love you," it said, "I love you": he would batter his way into heaven, he would tear delight from wherever delight might be—or else, and this was harder, a trembling man pleading, "Aid me or I perish," and it is woman's instinct not to let a man perish. "If I help you, I hurt myself," she sighed; and, "Hurt yourself, then," sighed the man; "would you have me perish. . .?"

So the owner by purchase smiled—

"You are mine," said he, "altogether mine, no one else has a lien upon you. When the weather is fine I will take you for drives in the sunshine. In the nights we will go to the opera, hearkening together to the tenor telling his sweet romanza, and when the wintry rain beats on the windows you will play the piano for me, and so we will be happy."

When he was quite recovered he went back to his office, and

found that one of his clerks had not arrived—this angered him; when he returned home again in the evening, he found that his wife was not there. So things go.

James Stephens

II

He was one of those who shy at the *tete-a-tete* life which, for a long time, matrimony demands. As his wedding-day appro- ached he grew fearful of the prolonged conversation which would stretch from the day of marriage, down the interm- inable vistas, to his death, and, more and more, he became doubtful of his ability to cope with, or his endurance to withstand, the extraordinary debate called marriage.

He was naturally a silent man. He did not dislike conversation if it was kept within decent limits: indeed, he responded to it contentedly enough, but when he had spoken or been addressed for more than an hour he became, first, impatient, then bored, and, finally, sulky or ill-mannered.—"With men," said he, "one can talk or be silent as one wishes, for between them there is a community of understanding which turns the occasional silence into a pregnant and fruitful interlude wherein a thought may keep itself warm until it is wanted: but with a woman!"—he could not pursue that speculation further, for his acquaintance with the sex was limited.

In every other respect his bride was a happiness. Her good looks soothed and pleased him. The touch of her hand gave him an extraordinary pleasure which concealed within it a yet more extraordinary excitement. Her voice, as a mere sound, enchanted him. It rippled and flowed, deepened and tinkled. It cooed and sang to him at times like the soft ringdove calling to its mate, and, at times again, it gurgled and piped like a thrush happy in the sunlight. The infinite variation of her tone astonished and delighted him, and if it could have remained something as dexterous and impersonal as a wind he would have been content to listen to it for ever—but, could he give her pipe for pipe? Would the rich gurgle or the soft coo sound at last as a horrid iteration, a mere clamour to which he must not only give an obedient heed, but must even answer from a head wherein silence had so peacefully brooded?

His mind was severe, his utterance staccato, and he had no knowledge of those conversational arts whereby nouns and verbs are amazingly transfigured into a gracious frolic or an intellectual pleasure. To snatch the chatter from its holder, toss and keep it playing in the air until another snatched it from him; to pluck a theory hot from the stating, and expand it until it was as iridescent and, perhaps, as thin as a soap-bubble: to light up and vivify a weighty conversation until the majestic thing sparkled and glanced like a jewel—these things he could not do, and he knew it. Many a time he had sat, amazed as at an exhibition of acrobatics, while around him the chatter burst and sang and shone. He had tried to bear his part, but had never been able to edge more than one word into that tossing cataract, and so he fell to the habit of listening instead of speaking.

With some reservations, he enjoyed listening, but particularly he enjoyed listening to his own thoughts as they trod slowly, but very certainly, to foregone conclusions. Into the silent arena of his mind no impertinent chatter could burst with a mouthful of puns or ridicule, or a reminiscence caught on the wing and hurled apropos to the very centre of discussion. His own means of conveying or gathering information was that whereby one person asked a question and another person answered it, and, if the subject proved deeper than the assembled profundity, then one pulled out the proper volume of an encyclopaedia, and the pearl was elicited as with a pin.

Meanwhile, his perturbation was real. There are people to whom we need not talk—let them pass: we overlook or smile distantly at the wretches, retaining our reputation abroad and our self-respect in its sanctuary: but there are others with whom we may not be silent, and into this latter category a wife enters with assured emphasis. He foresaw endless opportunities for that familiar discussion to which he was a stranger. There were breakfast-tables, dinner-tables, tea-tables, and, between these, there might be introduced those preposterous other tables which women invent for no purpose unless it be that of making talk. His own breakfast, dinner, and tea-tables had been solitary ones, whereat he lounged with a newspaper propped against a lamp, or a book resting one end against the sugar-bowl and the other against his plate.—This quietude would be ravaged from him for ever, and that tumult nothing could exorcise or impede. Further than these, he foresaw an interminable drawing-room, long walks together, and other, even more confidential and particular, sequestrations.

After one has married a lady, what does one say to her? He could not conceive any one saying anything beyond "Good-morning." Then the other aspect arrested him, "What does a woman find to say to a man?" Perhaps safety lay in this direction, for they were reputed notable and tireless speakers to whom replies are not pressingly necessary. He looked upon his sweetheart as from a distance, and tried to reconstruct her recent conversations.—He was amazed at the little he could remember. "I, I, I, we, we, we, this shop, that shop, Aunt Elsa, and chocolates." She had mentioned all these things on the previous day, but she did not seem to have said anything memorable about them, and, so far as he could recollect, he had said nothing in reply but "Oh, yes" and "To be sure!" Could he sustain a lifetime of small-talk on these meagre responses? He saw in vision his most miserable tea-table—a timid husband and a mad wife glaring down their noses at plates. The picture leaped at him as from a cinematograph and appalled him. . . . After a time they would not even dare to look at each other. Hatred would crouch behind these figures, waiting for its chain to be loosed!

So he came to the knowledge that he, so soon to be a husband, had been specially fashioned by nature to be a bachelor. For him safety lay in solitude: others, less rigorously planned, might safely venture into the haphazard, gregarious state of wedlock, but he not only could not, but must not, do so, and he meditated an appeal to his bride to release him from the contract. Several times the meditation almost became audible, but always, just as he toppled on the surge of speech, the dear lady loosed a torrent of irrelevancies which swirled him from all anchorage, and left him at the last stranded so distantly from his thought that he did not know how to find his way back to it.

It would be too brutally direct to shatter information about silk at one shilling the yard with a prayer for matrimonial freedom. The girl would be shocked—he could see her—she would stare at him, and suddenly grow red in the face and stammer; and he would be forced to trail through a lengthy, precise explanation of this matter which was not at all precise to himself. Furthermore, certain obscure emotions rendered him unwilling to be sundered from this girl.—There was the touch of her hand; more, the touch of her lips given bravely and with ready modesty—a contact not lightly to be relinquished. He did not believe he could ever weary of looking at her eyes: they were grey, widely open, and of a kindness such as he could not disbelieve in; a radiant cordiality, a soft, limpid goodwill; believing and trustful eyes which held no guile when they looked at him: there were her movements, her swiftness, spaciousness, her buoyant certainty: one remembered her hair, her hands, the way she wore a frock, and a strange, seductive something about the look of her shoe.

The thing was not possible! It is the last and darkest insult to tell the woman who loves you that you do not wish to marry her. Her indignant curiosity may be appeased only by the excuse that you like some other woman better, and although she may hate the explanation she will understand it—but no less legitimate excuse than this may pass sunderingly between a man and a woman.

It lay, therefore, that he must amend his own hand, and, accordingly, for the purpose of marital intercourse, he began a sad inquiry into the nature of things. The world was so full of things: clouds and winds and sewing machines, kings and brigands, hats and heads, flower-pots, jam and public-houses—surely one could find a little to chat about at any moment if one were not ambitiously particular. With inanimate objects one could speak of shape and colour and usefulness. Animate objects had, beside these, movements and aptitudes for eating and drinking, playing and quarrelling. Artistic things were well or badly executed, and were also capable of an inter-comparison which could not but be interesting and lengthy.—These things could all be talked about. There were positive and negative qualities attaching to everything, and when the former was exhausted the latter could still be profitably mined—"Order," said he, "subsists in everything, and even conversation must be subject to laws capable of ascertainment."

He carefully, and under the terms of badinage, approached other men, inquiring how they bore themselves in the matrimonial dispute, and what were the subjects usually spoken of in the intimacies of family life. But from these people he received the smallest assistance.—Some were ribald, some jocose, some so darkly explanatory that intelligence could not peer through the mist or could only divine that these hated their wives. One man held that all domestic matters should be left entirely to the wife and that talking was a domestic matter. Another said that the words "yes, no, and why" would safeguard a man through any labyrinth, however tortuous. Another said that he always went out when the wife began to speak; and yet another suggested that the only possible basis for conversation was that of perpetual opposition, where an affirmation was always countered by a denial, and the proving of the case exercised both time and intelligence.

As he sat in the train beside his wife the silence which he so dreaded came upon them. Emptiness buzzed in his head. He sought diligently for something to speak about—the character-ristics of objects! There were objects and to spare, but he could not say—"that window is square, it is made of glass," or, "the roof of this carriage is flat, it is made of wood."

Suddenly his wife buried her face in her muff, and her shoulders were convulsed. . . .

Love and contrition possessed him on the instant. He eased his husky throat, and the dreaded, interminable conversation began—

"What are you crying for, my dear?" said he.

Her voice, smothered by the fur, replied—

"I am not crying, darling," said she, "I am only laughing."

James Stephens

III

He got stiffly up from his seat before the fire—

"Be hanged," said he, "if I wait any longer for her. If she doesn't please to come in before this hour let her stop out." He stared into the fire for a few moments—"Let her go to Jericho," said he, and he tramped up to bed.

They had been married just six months, after, as he put it, the hardest courtship a man ever undertook. She was more like a piece of quicksilver than a girl. She was as uncertain as a spring wind, as flighty as a ball of thistledown—"Doesn't know her own mind for ten minutes together," he groaned. "Hasn't any mind at all," he'd think an hour later. While, on the following day, it might be—"That woman is too deep, she is dodging all round me, she is sticking her finger in my eye. She treats me as if I wasn't there at one moment, and diddles me as if I was Tom Fool the next—I'll get out of it."

He had got out of it three or four times—halted her against a wall, and, with a furious forefinger, wagged all her misdeeds in her face; then, rating her up, down and round, he had prepared to march away complacent and refreshed like Justice taking leave of a sinner, only to find that if the jade wept he could not go away—

"Dash it all," said he, "you can't leave a girl squatting down against a wall, with her head in her lap and she crying. Hang it," said he, "you feel as if there was water round your legs and you'll splash if you move."

So he leavened justice with mercy, and, having dried her tears with his lips, he found himself in the same position as before, with a mad suspicion tattering through his brain that maybe he had been "diddled" again.

But he married her, and to do that was a job also. She shied at matrimony. She shied at everything that looked plain or straight. She was like a young dog out for a walk: when she met a side-street she bolted down it and was instantly surrounded by adventure and misery, returning, like the recovered pup, thick with the mud of those excursions. There was a lust in her blood for side-streets, laneways and corners.

"Marriage!" said she, and she was woebegone—"Marriage will be for ever."

"So will heaven," he retorted comfortingly.

"So will—the other place," said she, with a giggle, and crushed him under the feeling that she envisaged him as the devil of that particular Hades, instead of as an unfortunate sinner plucked up by the heels and soused into the stew-pan by his wife.

He addressed himself—

"When we are married," said he, "I'll keep a hand on you, my lady, that you won't be able to wriggle away from. If you are slippery, and faith you are, why I'm tough, and so you'll find it." "Get rid of your kinks before you marry," said he. "I've no use for a wife with one eye on me, and it a dubious one, and the other one squinting into a parlour two streets off. You've got to settle down and quit tricks. A wife has no one else to deceive but her husband, that's all she can want tricks for, and there's not going to be any in my house. It's all right for a pretty girl to be a bit larky—"

"Am I really pretty?" said she, deeply interested and leaning forward with her hands clasping her knees—"Do you really and truly think I am pretty? I met a man one time, he had a brown moustache and blue eyes, outside a tailor's shop in Georges Street, with a public-house on one side, and he said he thought I was very pretty: he told me what his name was, but I forget it: maybe, you know him: he wears a tweed suit with a

James Stephens

stripe and a soft hat—Let me see, no, his name began with a T—"

"His name was Thief," he roared, "and that was his profession too. Don't let me catch you talking with a strange man, or you'll get hurt, and his brown eyes will be mixed up with his blue moustache."

So married they were, six months now, and the wits were nearly worried out of him in trying to keep pace with his wife's vagaries. Matrimony had not cured her love for side-streets, short cuts and chance acquaintances, and she was gradually making her husband travel at a similar tangent. When they started to go to church he would find, to his amazement, that they were in the Museum. If they journeyed with a Museum for an objective they were certain to pull up in the Botanic Gardens. A call on a friend usually turned into a visit to a theatre or a walk by the Dodder—

"Heart-scalded I am," said he, "with her hopping and trotting. She travels sideways like a crab, so she does. She has a squint in her walk. Her boots have a bias outwards. I'm getting bow-legged, so I am, slewing round corners after her. I'll have to put my foot down," said he.

And now it was all finished. Here was twelve o'clock at night and an absent wife—a detestable combination. Twelve o'clock at night outside a house is an immoral hour, inside a house it is non-moral, but respectable. There is nothing in the street at that time but dubiety. Who would be a husband listening through the tolling of midnight for a muffled footfall?—And he had told her not to go: had given an order, formulated his imperative and inflexible will—

"Never mind! I'll stand by it," said he, "this is the last straw. One break and then freedom. Surgery is better than tinkering. Cut the knot and let who will try to join it then. One pang, and afterwards ease, fresh air, and freedom: fresh air! gulps of it, with the head back and an easy mind. I'm not the man to be fooled for ever—surgery! surgery!"

His wife had wished to see a friend that night and requested her husband to go with her—he refused—

"You're always trapsin about," said he.

She entreated.

He heaved an angry forehead at her, puckered an eye, toned a long No that wagged vibration behind it like an undocked tail.

She persisted, whereupon he loosed his thunder—

"You're not to step outside the house this night, ma'am," said he; and to her angry "I will go," he barked, "If you do go, don't come back here. I'll have a dutiful wife or I'll have none—stay in or stay out. I'm tired humouring your whimsies, let you humour mine now—"

Then a flame gathered on her face, it grew hot in her voice, flashed to a point in her eyes—

"I'm going out to-night," said she loudly; "are you coming with me?"

"I'm not," said he.

"Then," she snapped, "I'll go by myself."

"Wherever you go to-night you can stay," he roared. "Don't come back to this house."

"I'm not mad enough to want to," she replied. "I wish I'd never seen your old house. I wish I'd never seen yourself. You are just as dull as your house is, and nearly as flat. It's a stupid, uninteresting, slow house, so it is, and you are a stupid, dissatisfied grump of a man, so you are. I'd sooner live in a cave with a hairy bear, so I would—" and out she ran.

Two minutes later he had heard the door bang, and then silence.

That was five hours ago, and during all these long hours he had sat staring sourly into the fire, seeing goodness knows what burnt-up visions therein, waiting to hear a footfall, and an entreating voice at the key-hole; apologies and tears perhaps, and promises of amendment. Now it was after twelve o'clock, darkness everywhere and silence. Time and again a policeman's tramp or the hasty, light footfall of adventure went by. So he stood up at last sour and vindictive—

"She would have her fling. She wouldn't give in. She doesn't care a tinker's curse what I say. . . . Let her go to Jericho," said he, and he tramped up to bed.

In his bedroom he did not trouble to get a light. He undressed in a bitterly savage mood and rolled into bed, only to jump out again in sudden terror, for there was some one in it. It was his wife. He lay down with a hazy, half-mad mind. Had he wronged her? Was she more amenable than he had fancied? She had not gone out at all—or, had she gone out, sneaked in again by the back door and crept noiselessly to bed. . . .?

He fell asleep at last on the tattered fringe of a debate—Had he wronged her? or had she diddled him again?

A GLASS OF BEER

It was now his custom to sit there. The world has its habits, why should a man not have his? The earth rolls out of light and into darkness as punctually as a business man goes to and from his office; the seasons come with the regularity of automata, and go as if they were pushed by an ejector; so, night after night, he strolled from the Place de l'Observatoire to the Font St. Michel, and, on the return journey, sat down at the same Cafe, at the same table, if he could manage it, and ordered the same drink.

So regular had his attendance become that the waiter would suggest the order before it was spoken. He did not drink beer because he liked it, but only because it was not a difficult thing to ask for. Always he had been easily discouraged, and he distrusted his French almost as much as other people had reason to. The only time he had varied the order was to request "un vin blanc gommee," but on that occasion he had been served with a postage stamp for twenty-five centimes, and he still wondered when he remembered it.

He liked to think of his first French conversation. He wanted something to read in English, but was timid of asking for it. He walked past all the newspaper kiosks on the Boulevard, anxiously scanning the vendors inside—they were usually very stalwart, very competent females, who looked as though they had outgrown their sins but remembered them with pleasure. They had the dully-polished, slightly-battered look of a modern antique. The words "M'sieu, Madame" rang from them as from bells. They were very alert, sitting, as it were, on tiptoe, and their eyes hit one as one approached. They were like spiders squatting in their little houses waiting for their daily flies.

He found one who looked jolly and harmless, sympathetic indeed, and to her, with a flourished hat, he approached. Said he, "Donnez-moi, Madame, s'il vous plait, le *Daily Mail*." At the second repetition the good lady smiled at him, a smile compounded of benevolence and comprehension, and instantly, with a "V'la M'sieu," she handed him *The New York Herald*. They had saluted each other, and he marched down the road in delight, with his first purchase under his arm and his first foreign conversation accomplished.

At that time everything had delighted him—the wide, well-lighted Boulevard, the concierges knitting in their immense doorways, each looking like a replica of the other, each seeming sister to a kiosk-keeper or a cat. The exactly-courteous speech of the people and their not quite so rigorously courteous manners pleased him. He listened to the voluble men who went by, speaking in a haste so breathless that he marvelled how the prepositions and conjunctions stuck to their duty in so swirling an ocean of chatter. There was a big black dog with a mottled head who lay nightly on the pavement opposite the Square de l'Observatoire. At intervals he raised his lean skull from the ground and composed a low lament to an absent friend. His grief was respected. The folk who passed stepped sidewards for him, and he took no heed of their passage—a lonely, introspective dog to whom a caress or a bone were equally childish things: Let me alone, he seemed to say, I have my grief, and it is company enough. There was the very superior cat who sat on every window-ledge, winking at life. He (for in France all cats are masculine by order of philology), he did not care a rap for man or dog, but he liked women and permitted them to observe him. There was the man who insinuated himself between the tables at the Cafe, holding out postcard-representations of the Pantheon, the Louvre, Notre Dame, and other places. From beneath these cards his dexterous little finger would suddenly flip others. One saw a hurried leg, an arm that shone and vanished, a bosom that fled shyly again, an audacious swan, a Leda who was thoroughly enjoying herself and had never heard of virtue. His look suggested that he thought better of one than to suppose that one was not interested in the nude. "M'sieu," he seemed to say, with his fixed, brown-eyed regard, "this is indeed a leg, an authentic leg, not disguised by even the littlest of stockings; it is arranged precisely as M'sieu would desire it." His sorrow as he went away was dignified with regret for an inartistic gentleman. One was *en garcon*, and yet one would not look at one's postcards! One had better then cease to be an artist and take to peddling onions and asparagus as the vulgar do.

It was all a long time ago, and now, somehow, the savour had departed from these things. Perhaps he had seen them too often. Perhaps a kind of public surreptitiousness, a quite open furtiveness, had troubled him. Maybe he was not well. He sat at his Cafe, three quarters down the Boulevard, and before him a multitude of grotesque beings were pacing as he sipped his bock.

Good manners decreed that he should not stare too steadfastly, and he was one who obeyed these delicate dictations. Alas! he was one who obeyed all dictates. For him authority wore a halo, and many sins which his heyday ought to have committed had been left undone only because they were not sanctioned by immediate social usage. He was often saddened when he thought of the things he had not done. It was the only sadness to which he had access, because the evil deeds which he had committed were of so tepid and hygienic a character that they could not be mourned for without hypocrisy, and now that he was released from all privileged restraints and overlookings and could do whatever he wished he had no wish to do anything.

His wife had been dead for over a year. He had hungered, he had prayed for her death. He had hated that woman (and for how many years!) with a kind of masked ferocity. How often he had been tempted to kill her or to kill himself! How often he had dreamed that she had run away from him or that he had run away from her! He had invented Russian Princes, and Music Hall Stars, and American Billionaires with whom she could adequately elope, and he had both loved and loathed the prospect. What unending, slow quarrels they had together! How her voice had droned pitilessly on his ears! She in one room, he in another, and through the open door there rolled that unending recitation of woes and reproaches, an inter-minable catalogue of nothings, while he sat dumb as a fish, with a mind that smouldered or blazed. He had stood unseen with a hammer, a poker, a razor in his hand, on tiptoe to do it. A movement, a rush, one silent rush and it was done! He had revelled in her murder. He had caressed it, rehearsed it, relished it, had jerked her head back, and hacked, and listened to her entreaties bubbling through blood!

And then she died! When he stood by her bed he had wished to taunt her, but he could not do it. He read in her eyes—I am dying, and in a little time I shall have vanished like dust on the wind, but you will still be here, and you will never see me again—He wished to ratify that, to assure her that it was actually so, to say that he would come home on the morrow night, and she would not be there, and that he would return home every night, and she would never be there. But he could not say it. Somehow the words, although he desired them, would not come. His arm went to her neck and settled there. His hand caressed her hair, her cheek. He kissed her eyes, her lips, her languid hands; and the words that came were only an infantile babble of regrets and apologies, assurances that he did love her, that he had never loved any one before, and never would love any one again. . . .

Every one who passed looked into the Cafe where he sat. Every one who passed looked at him. There were men with sallow faces and wide black hats. Some had hair that flapped about them in the wind, and from their locks one gathered, with some distaste, the spices of Araby. Some had cravats that fluttered and fell and rose again like banners in a storm. There were men with severe, spade-shaped, most responsible-looking beards, and quizzical little eyes which gave the lie to their hairy sedateness—eyes which had spent long years in looking sidewards as a woman passed. There were men of every stage of foppishness—men who had spent so much time on their moustaches that they had only a little left for their finger-nails, but their moustaches exonerated them; others who were coated to happiness, trousered to grotesqueness, and booted to misery. He thought—In this city the men wear their own coats, but they all wear some one else's trousers, and their boots are syndicated.

He saw no person who was self-intent. They were all deeply conscious, not of themselves, but of each other. They were all looking at each other. They were all looking at him; and he returned the severe, or humourous, or appraising gaze of each with a look nicely proportioned to the passer, giving back exactly what was given to him, and no more. He did not stare, for nobody stared. He just looked and looked away, and was as mannerly as was required.

A negro went by arm in arm with a girl who was so sallow that she was only white by courtesy. He was a bulky man, and as he bent greedily over his companion it was evident that to him she was whiter than the snow of a single night.

Women went past in multitudes, and he knew the appearance of them all. How many times he had watched them or their duplicates striding and mincing and bounding by, each moving like an animated note of interrogation! They were long, and medium, and short. There were women of a thinness beyond comparison, sheathed in skirts as featly as a rapier in a scabbard. There were women of a monumental, a mighty fatness, who billowed and rolled in multitudinous, stormy garments. There were slow eyes that drooped on one heavily as a hand, and quick ones that stabbed and withdrew, and glanced again appealingly, and slid away cursing. There were some who lounged with a false sedateness, and some who fluttered in an equally false timidity. Some wore velvet shoes without heels. Some had shoes, the heels whereof were of such inordinate length that the wearers looked as though they were perched on stilts and would topple to perdition if their skill failed for an instant. They passed and they looked at him; and from each, after the due regard, he looked away to the next in interminable procession.

There were faces also to be looked at: round chubby faces wherefrom the eyes of oxen stared in slow, involved rumination. Long faces that were keener than hatchets and as cruel. Faces that pretended to be scornful and were only piteous. Faces contrived to ape a temperament other than their own. Raddled faces with heavy eyes and rouged lips. Ragged lips that had been chewed by every mad dog in the world. What lips there were everywhere! Bright scarlet splashes in dead-white faces. Thin red gashes that suggested rat-traps instead of kisses. Bulbous, flabby lips that would wobble and shiver if attention failed them. Lips of a horrid fascination that one looked at and hated and ran to. . . . Looking at him slyly or boldly, they passed along, and turned after a while and repassed him, and turned again in promenade.

He had a sickness of them all. There had been a time when these were among the things he mourned for not having done, but that time was long past. He guessed at their pleasures, and knew them to be without salt. Life, said he, is as unpleasant as a plate of cold porridge. Somehow the world was growing empty for him. He wondered was he outgrowing his illusions, or his appetites, or both? The things in which other men took such interest were drifting beyond him, and (for it seemed that the law of compensation can fail) nothing was drifting towards him in recompense. He foresaw himself as a box with nothing inside it, and he thought—It is not through love or fear or distress that men commit suicide: it is because they have become empty: both the gods and the devils have deserted them and they can no longer support that solemn stagnation. He marvelled to see with what activity men and women played the most savourless of games! With what zest of pursuit they tracked what petty interests. He saw them as ants scurrying with scraps of straw, or apes that pick up and drop and pick again, and he marvelled from what fount they renewed themselves, or with what charms they exorcised the demons of satiety.

On this night life did not seem worth while. The taste had gone from his mouth; his bock was water vilely coloured; his cigarette was a hot stench. And yet a full moon was peeping in the trees along the path, and not far away, where the countryside bowed in silver quietude, the rivers ran through undistinguishable fields chanting their lonely songs. The seas leaped and withdrew, and called again to the stars, and gathered in ecstasy and roared skywards, and the trees did not rob each other more than was absolutely necessary. The men and women were all hidden away, sleeping in their cells, where the moon could not see them, nor the clean wind, nor the stars. They were sundered for a little while from their eternal arithmetic. The grasping hands were lying as quietly as the paws of a sleeping dog. Those eyes held no further speculation than the eyes of an ox who lies down. The tongues that had lied all day, and been treacherous and obscene and respectful by easy turn, said nothing more; and he thought it was very good that they were all hidden, and that for a little time the world might swing darkly with the moon in its own wide circle and its silence.

He paid for his bock, gave the waiter a tip, touched his hat to a lady by sex and a gentleman by clothing, and strolled back to his room that was little, his candle that was three-quarters consumed, and his picture which might be admired when he was dead but which he would never be praised for painting; and, after sticking his foot through the canvas, he tugged himself to bed, agreeing to commence the following morning just as he had the previous one, and the one before that, and the one before that again.

James Stephens

ONE AND ONE

Do you hate me, you!
Sitting quietly there,
With the burnished hair
That frames the two
Deep eyes of your face
In a smooth embrace.

And you say naught,
And I never speak;
But you rest your cheek
On your hand, a thought
Showing plain as the brow
Goes wrinkling now.

Of what do you think,
Sitting opposite me,
As you stir the tea
That you do not drink,
And frown at nought
With those brows of thought.

THREE WOMEN WHO WEPT

He was one of those men who can call ladies by their Christian names. One day he met twenty-four duchesses walking on a red carpet, and he winked at them, and they were all delighted. It was so at first he appeared to her. Has a mere girl any protection against a man of that quality? and she was the very merest of girls—she knew it. It was not that she was ignorant, for she had read widely about men, and she had three brothers as to whom she knew divers intimate things.

The girl who has been reared among brothers has few defences against other males. She has acquired two things—a belief in the divine right of man, and a curiosity as to what those men are like who are not her brothers. She may love her brothers, but she cannot believe that they adequately represent the other sex. Does not every girl wish to marry the antithesis of her brother? The feeling is that one should marry as far outside of the family as is possible, and as far outside of one's self as may be; but love has become subject to geography, and our choice is often bounded by the tramline upon which we travel from our houses to our businesses and back again.

While she loved and understood her brothers, she had not in the least understood or believed in the stories she had read, and so, when the Young Man out of a Book came to her, she was delighted but perplexed.It was difficult to live up to him worthily. It was difficult to know what he would do next, and it was exceedingly difficult to keep out of his way; for, indeed, he seemed to pervade the part of the world where she lived. He

James Stephens

was as ubiquitous as the air or the sky. If she went into a shop, he was pacing on the pavement when she came out. If she went for a walk he was standing at the place farther than which she had decided not to go. She had found him examining a waterfall on the Dodder, leaning over the bear-pit in the Zoological Gardens, and kneeling beside her in the Chapel, and her sleep had been distressed by the reflection that maybe he was sitting on her window-sill like a sad sparrow drenched in the rain, all its feathers on end with the cold, and its eyes wide open staring at misery. The first time they met he spoke to her. He plucked a handkerchief from somewhere and thrust it into her hand, saying—

"You have dropped this, I think"—and she had been too alarmed to disown it.

It was a mighty handkerchief. It was so big that it would scarcely fit into her muff.—"It is a table-cloth," said she, as she solemnly stuffed away its lengthy flaps. "It is his own," she thought a moment later, and she would have laughed like a mad woman, only that she had no time, for he was pacing delicately by her side, and talking in a low voice that was partly a whisper and partly a whistle, and was entirely and disturbingly delicious.

The next time they met very suddenly. Scarcely a dozen paces separated them. She could see him advancing towards her, and knew by his knitted brows that he was searching anxiously for something to say. When they drew together he lifted his hat and murmured—

"How is your handkerchief to-day?"

The query so astonished her that (the verb is her own) she simply bawled with laughter. From that moment he treated her with freedom, for if once you laugh with a person you admit him to equality, you have ranked him definitely as a vertebrate, your hand is his by right of species, scarcely can you withhold even your lips from his advances. Another, a strange, a fascinating thing, was that he was afraid of her. It was inconceivable, it was mad, but it was true. He looked at her with disguised terror. His bravado was the slenderest mask. Every word he said was uttered tentatively, it was subject to her approval, and if she opposed a statement he dropped it instantly and adopted her alternative as one adopts a gift. This astonished her who had been prepared to be terrified. He kept a little distance between them as he walked, and when she looked at him he looked away. She had a vision of herself as an ogre—whiskers sprouted all over her face, her ears bulged and swaggled, her voice became a cavernous rumble, her conversation sounded like fee-faw-fum—and yet, her brothers were not afraid of her in the least; they pinched her and kicked her hat.

He spoke (but always without prejudice) of the loveliest things imaginable—matters about which brothers had no conception, and for which they would not have any reverence. He said one day that the sky was blue, and, on looking she found that it was so. The sky was amazingly blue. It had never struck her before, but there was a colour in the firmament before which one might fall down and worship. Sunlight was not the hot glare which it had been: it was rich, generous, it was inexpressibly beautiful. The colour and scent of flowers became more varied. The world emerged as from shrouds and cerements. It was tender and radiant, comeliness lived everywhere, and goodwill. Laughter! the very ground bubbled with it: the grasses waved their hands, the trees danced and curtsied to one another with gentle dignity, and the wind lurched down the path with its hat on the side of its head and its hands in its pockets, whistling like her younger brother.

And then he went away. She did not see him any more. He was not by the waterfall on the Dodder, nor hanging over the bear-pit in the Zoo. He was not in the Chapel, nor on the pavement when she came out of a shop. He was not anywhere. She searched, but he was not anywhere. And the sun became the hot pest it had always been: the heavens were stuffed with dirty clouds the way a second-hand shop is stuffed with dirty

James Stephens

bundles: the trees were hulking corner-boys with muddy boots: the wind blew dust into her eye, and her brothers pulled her hair and kicked her hat; so that she went apart from all these. She sat before the mirror regarding herself with woeful amazement—

"He was afraid of me!" she said.

And she wept into his monstrous handkerchief.

II

When he came into the world he came howling, and he howled without ceasing for seven long years, except at the times when he happened to be partaking of nourishment, or was fast asleep, and, even then, he snored with a note of defiance and protest which proved that his humour was not for peace.

The time came when he ceased to howl and became fascinated by the problem of how to make other people howl. In this art he became an adept. When he and another child chanced to be left together there came, apparently from the uttermost ends of the earth, a pin, and the other child and the pin were soon in violent and lamentable conjunction.

So he grew.

"Be hanged if I know what to do with him," said his father as he rebuckled on his belt. "The devil's self hasn't got the shape or match of such an imp in all the length and breadth of his seven hells. I'm sick, sore and sorry whacking him, so I am, and before long I'll be hung on the head of him. I'm saying that there's more deceit and devilment in his bit of a carcass than there is in a public-house full of tinkers, so there is."

He turned to his wife—

"It's no credit at all the son you've bore me, ma'am, but a sorrow and a woe that'll be killing us in our old age and maybe damning our souls at the heel of it. Where he got his blackguardly ways from I'm not saying, but it wasn't from my side of the house anyway, so it wasn't, and that's a moral. Get out of my sight you sniffling lout, and if ever I catch you at your practices again I'll lam you till you won't be able to wink without help, so I will."

"Musha," sobbed his wife, "don't be always talking out of you.

Any one would think that it was an old, criminal thief you were instructing, instead of a bit of a child that'll be growing out of his wildness in no time. Come across to me, child, come over to your mother, my lamb."

That night, when his father got into bed, he prodded his foot against something under the sheets. Investigation discovered a brown paper bag at the end of the bed. A further search revealed a wasp's nest, inside of which there was an hundred angry wasps blazing for combat. His father left the room with more expedition than decency. He did not stop to put on as much as his hat. He fled to the stream which ran through the meadow at the back of their house, and lay down in it, and in two seconds there was more bad language than water in the stream. Every time he lifted his head for air the wasps flew at him with their tails curled. They kept him there for half an hour, and in that time he laid in the seeds of more rheumatism than could be cured in two lifetimes.

When he returned home he found his wife lying on the floor with a blanket wrapped about her head, groaning by instinct, for she was senseless.

Her face had disappeared. There was nothing where it had been but poisoned lumps. A few days later it was found that she was blind of one eye, and there was danger of erysipelas setting in.

The boy could not be found for some time, but a neighbour, observing a stone come from nowhere in particular and hit a cat, located the first cause in a ditch. He brought the boy home, and grabbed his father just in time to prevent murder being done.

It was soon found that the only thing which eased the restless moaning woman was the touch of her son. All her unmanageable, delirious thoughts centred on him—

"Sure he's only a boy; beating never did good to anything.

Give him a chance now for wouldn't a child be a bit wild anyhow. You will be a good boy, won't you? Come to your mother, my lamb."

So the lad grew, from twelve to fifteen, from fifteen to twenty. Soon he attained to manhood. To his mother he seemed to have leaped in a day from the careless, prattling babe to the responsibly-whiskered miracle at whom mothers sit and laugh in secret delight. This towering, big-footed, hairy person! was he really the little boy who used to hide in her skirts when his father scowled? She had only to close her eyes and she could feel again a pair of little hands clawing at her breast, sore from the violent industry of soft, wee lips.

So he grew. Breeches that were big became small. Bony wrists were continually pushing out of coat cuffs. His feet would burst out of his boots. He grew out of everything but one. A man may outgrow his breeches, he cannot outgrow his nature: his body is never too big or too small to hold that.

Every living thing in the neighbourhood knew him. When a cat saw him coming it climbed a tree and tried to look as much like a lump of wood as it could. When a dog heard his step it tucked its tail out of sight and sought for a hole in the hedge. The birds knew he carried stones in his pockets. No tree cast so black a shadow in the sunlight as he did. There were stories of a bottle of paraffin oil and a cat that screeched in flames. Folk told of a maltreated dog that pointed its nose to heaven and bayed a curse against humanity until a terrified man battered it to death with a shovel. No one knew who did it, but every one said there were only two living hearts capable of these iniquities—one belonged to the devil, the other to our young man, and they acquitted Satan of the deeds.

The owner of the dog swore by the beasts in the field and the stars in the sky that he would tear the throat of the man who had injured his beast.

The father drove his one-eyed wife from the house, and went

James Stephens

with her to live elsewhere; but she left him and went back to her son, and her husband forswore the twain.

When women saw him in the road they got past him with their breath hissing through their teeth in fear. When men passed him they did it warily, with their fists clenched and their eyes alert. He was shunned by every one. The strength of his arms also was a thing to be afraid of, and in the world there was but two welcomes for him, one from his mother, the other from an old, grey rat that slept in his breast—

"Sure, you're all against him," his mother would say. "Why don't you give the boy a chance? It's only the hot blood of youth that's working in him—and he never did it either. Look how kind he is to me! never the bad word or the hard look! Ye black hearts that blame my boy, look among yourselves for the villain. No matter who is against you, come to your mother, my lamb."

He was found one day at the foot of the cliff with his neck broken. Some said that he had slipped and fallen, some said he had committed suicide, other some pursed their lips tightly and said nothing. All were relieved that he was gone, saving his mother only, she mourned for her only son, and wept bitterly, refusing to be comforted until she died.

III

She had begun to get thin. Her face was growing sharp and peaked. The steady curve of her cheek had become a little indeterminate. Her chin had begun to sag and her eyes to look a little weary. But she had not observed these things, for we do not notice ourselves very much until some other person thinks we are worthy of observation and tells us so; and these changes are so gradual and tiny that we seldom observe them until we awaken for a moment or two in our middle age and then we get ready to fall asleep again.

When her uncle died, the solicitors who had administered his will handed her a small sum of money and intimated that from that date she must hew out her own path in life, and as she had most of the household furniture of her late uncle at her disposal, she decided to let lodgings. Setting about that end with all possible expedition she finished writing "apartments to let" on a square of pasteboard, and, having placed it prominently in a window, she folded her mittened hands and sat down with some trepidation to await the advent of a lodger.

He came in the night time with the stars and the moon. He was running like a youthful god, she thought, for her mind had not yet been weaned from certain vanities, and she could not see that a gigantic policeman was in his wake, tracking him with elephantine bounds, and now and again snatching a gasp from hurry to blow furious warnings on a whistle.

It was the sound of the whistle which opened her eyes through her ears. She went to the door and saw him coming framed in the moonlight, his arms pressed tightly to his sides, his head well up and his feet kicking a mile a minute on the pavement. Behind him the whistle shrilled with angry alarm, and the thunder of monumental feet came near as the policeman sprinted in majesty.

As the lodger ran she looked at him. He was a long-legged,

young man with a pleasant, clean-shaven face. His eyes met hers, and, although he grinned anxiously, she saw that he was frightened. That frightened smile gripped her and she panted noiselessly, "Oh, run, run!"

As he drew level he fixed his gaze on her, and, stopping suddenly, he ducked under her arm and was inside the house in a twinkling.

The poor lady's inside curled up in fear and had started to uncurl in screams when she felt a hand laid gently on her arm, and, "Don't make a noise, or I'm caught," said a voice, whereupon, and with exceeding difficulty, she closed her mouth while the scream went sizzling through her teeth in little gasps. But now the enemy appeared round the corner, tooting incessantly on his whistle, and whacking sparks from the cobblestones as he ran. Behind her she could hear the laboured breathing of a spent runner. The lodger was kneeling at her skirts: he caught her hand and pressed his face against it entreatingly—

The policeman drew near—

"Did you see a fellow skedaddling along here, ma'am?" said he.

She hesitated for only a moment and then, pointing to a laneway opposite, replied—

"He went up there."

"Thank you, ma'am," said the policeman with a genial smile, and he sprinted up the laneway whistling cheerily.

She turned to the lodger—

"You had better go now," said she.

He looked at her ruefully and hesitated—

"If I go now," he replied, "I'll be caught and get a month. I'll have to eat skilly, you know, and pick oakum, and get my hair cut."

She looked at his hair—it was brown and wavy, just at his ears it crisped into tiny curls, and she thought it would be a great pity to cut it. He bore her scrutiny well, with just a trifle of embarrassment and a shyly humorous eye—

"You are the kindest woman I ever met," said he, "and I'll never forget you as long as I live. I'll go away now because I wouldn't like to get you into trouble for helping me."

"What did you do?" she faltered.

"I got into a fight with another man," he replied, "and while we were hammering each other the policeman came up. He was going to arrest me, and, before I knew what I was doing, I knocked him down."

She shook her head—

"You should not have done that. That was very wrong, for he was only doing his duty."

"I know it," he admitted, "but, do you see, I didn't know what I was doing, and then, when I hit him, I got frightened and ran."

"You poor boy," said she tenderly.

"And somehow, when I saw you, I knew you wouldn't give me up: wasn't it queer?"

What a nice, gentlemanly young fellow he is, she thought.

"But, of course, I cannot be trespassing on your kindness any longer," he continued, "so I'll leave at once, and if ever I get the chance to repay your kindness to a stranger—"

"Perhaps," said she, "it might not be quite safe for you to go yet. Come inside and I will give you a cup of tea. You must be worn out with the excitement and the danger. Why, you are shaking all over: a cup of tea will steady your nerves and give him time to stop looking for you."

"Perhaps," said he, "if I turned my coat inside out and turned my trousers up, they wouldn't notice me."

"We will talk it over," she replied with a wise nod.

That was how the lodger came. He told her his name and his employment—he was a bookmaker's clerk. He brought his luggage, consisting mostly of neckties, to her house the following day from his former lodgings—

"Had a terrible time getting away from them," said he. "They rather liked me, you know, and couldn't make out why I wanted to leave."

"As if you weren't quite free to do as you wished," quoth his indignant new landlady.

"And then, when they found I would go, they made me pay two weeks' rent in lieu of notice—mean, wasn't it?"

"The low people," she replied. "I will not ask you to pay anything this week."

He put his bandbox on the ground, and shook hands with her—

"You are a brick," said he, "the last and the biggest of them. There isn't the like of you in this or any other world, and never was and never will be, world without end, amen."

"Oh, don't say that," said she shyly.

"I will," he replied, "for it's the truth. I'll hire a sandwichman to stop people in the street and tell it to them. I'll get a week's engagement at the theatre and sing it from the stage. I'll make up a poem about your goodness. I don't know what to do to thank you. Do you see, if I had to pay you now I'd have to pawn something, and I really believe I have pawned everything they'd lend on to get the money for that two weeks' rent. I'm broke until Friday, that's my pay day, but that night I'll come home with my wages piled up on a cart."

"I can lend you a few shillings until then," said she laughing.

"Oh, no," said he. "It's not fair. I couldn't do that," but he could.

Well the light of the world shone out of the lodger. He was like a sea breeze in a soap factory. When he awakened in the morning he whistled. When he came down to breakfast he sang. When he came home in the evening he danced. He had an amazing store of vitality: from the highest hair on the top of his head down to his heels he was alive. His average language was packed with jokes and wonderful curses. He was as chatty as a girl, as good-humoured as a dog, as unconscious as a kitten—and she knew nothing at all of men, except, perhaps, that they wore trousers and were not girls. The only man with whom she had ever come in contact was her uncle, and he might have been described as a sniffy old man with a cold; a blend of gruel and grunt, living in an atmosphere of ointment and pills and patent medicine advertisements—and, behold, she was living in unthinkable intimacy with the youngest of young men; not an old, ache-ridden, cough-racked, corn-footed septuagenarian, but a young, fresh-faced, babbling rascal who laughed like the explosion of a blunderbuss, roared songs as long as he was within earshot and danced when he had nothing else to do. He used to show her how to do hand-balances on the arm-chair, and while his boots were cocked up in the air she would grow stiff with terror for his safety and for that of the adjacent crockery.

The first morning she was giving him his breakfast, intending afterwards to have her own meal in the kitchen, but he used language of such strangely attractive ferocity, and glared at her with such a humorously-mad eye that she was compelled to breakfast with him.

At night, when he returned to his tea, he swore by this and by that he would die of hunger unless she ate with him; and then he told her all the doings of the day, the bets that had been made and lost, and what sort of a man his boss was, and he extolled the goodness of his friends, and lectured on the vast iniquity of his enemies.

So things went until she was as intimate with him as if he had been her brother. One night he came home just a trifle tipsy. She noted at last what was wrong with him, and her heart yearned over the sinner. There were five or six glasses inside of him, and each was the father of an antic. He was an opera company, a gymnasium, and a menagerie at once, all tinged with a certain hilarious unsteadiness which was fascinating. But at last he got to his bed, which was more than she did.

She sat through the remainder of the night listening to the growth of her half-starved heart. Oh, but there was a warmth there now. . . .! Springtime and the moon in flood. What new leaves are these which the trees put forth? Bird, singing at the peep of morn, where gottest thou thy song? Be still, be still, thou stranger, fluttering a wing at my breast. . . .

At the end of a month the gods moved, and when the gods move they trample mortals in the dust.

The lodger's employer left Dublin for London, taking his clerk with him.

"Good-bye," said he.

"Good-bye," she replied, "and a pleasant journey to you."

And she took the card with "Apartments to Let" written upon

it and placed it carefully in the window, and then, folding her mittened hands, she sat down to await the coming of another lodger, and as she sat she wept bitterly.

THE TRIANGLE

Nothing is true for ever. A man and a fact will become equally decrepit and will tumble in the same ditch, for truth is as mortal as man, and both are outlived by the tortoise and the crow.

To say that two is company and three is a crowd is to make a very temporary statement. After a short time satiety or use and wont has crept sunderingly between the two, and, if they are any company at all, they are bad company, who pray discreetly but passionately for the crowd which is censured by the proverb.

If there had not been a serpent in the Garden of Eden it is likely that the bored inhabitants of Paradise would have been forced to import one from the outside wilds merely to relax the tedium of a too-sustained duet. There ought to be a law that when a man and a woman have been married for a year they should be forcibly separated for another year. In the meantime, as our law-givers have no sense, we will continue to invoke the serpent.

Mrs. Mary Morrissy had been married for quite a time to a gentleman of respectable mentality, a sufficiency of money, and a surplus of leisure—Good things? We would say so if we dared, for we are growing old and suspicious of all appearances, and we do not easily recognize what is bad or good. Beyond the social circumference we are confronted with a debatable ground where good and bad are so merged that we cannot distinguish the one from the other. To her husband's mental attainments (from no precipitate, dizzy peaks did he stare; it was only a tiny plain with the tiniest of hills in the centre) Mrs. Morrissy extended a courtesy entirely unmixed with awe. For his money she extended a hand which could still thrill to an unaccustomed prodigality, but for his leisure (and it was illimitable) she could find no possible use.

The quality of permanency in a transient world is terrifying. A permanent husband is a bore, and we do not know what to do with him. He cannot be put on a shelf. He cannot be hung on a nail. He will not go out of the house. There is no escape from him, and he is always the same. A smile of a certain dimension, moustaches of this inevitable measurement, hands that waggle and flop like those of automata—these are his. He eats this way and he drinks that way, and he will continue to do so until he stiffens into the ultimate quietude. He snores on this note, he laughs on that, dissonant, unescapeable, unchanging. This is the way he walks, and he does not know how to run. A predictable beast indeed! He is known inside and out, catalogued, ticketed, and he cannot be packed away.

Mrs. Morrissy did not yet commune with herself about it, but if her grievance was anonymous it was not unknown. There is a back-door to every mind as to every house, and although she refused it house-room, the knowledge sat on her very hearthstone whistling for recognition.

Indeed, she could not look anywhere without seeing her husband. He was included in every landscape. His moustaches and the sun rose together. His pyjamas dawned with the moon. When the sea roared so did he, and he whispered with the river and the wind. He was in the picture but was out of drawing. He was in the song but was out of tune. He agitated her dully, surreptitiously, unceasingly. She questioned of space in a whisper, "Are we glued together?" said she. There was a bee in a flower, a burly rascal who did not care a rap for any one: he sat enjoying himself in a scented and gorgeous palace, and in him she confided:

"If," said she to the bee, "if that man doesn't stop talking to me I'll kick him. I'll stick a pin in him if he does not go out for a walk."

She grew desperately nervous. She was afraid that if she looked at him any longer she would see him. To-morrow, she thought, I may notice that he is a short, fat man in spectacles, and that will be the end of everything. But the end of everything is also the beginning of everything, and so she was one half in fear and the other half in hope. A little more and she would hate him, and would begin the world again with the same little hope and the same little despair for her meagre capital.

She had already elaborated a theory that man was intended to work, and that male sloth was offensive to Providence and should be forbidden by the law. At times her tongue thrilled, silently as yet, to certain dicta of the experienced Aunt who had superintended her youth, to the intent that a lazy man is a nuisance to himself and to everybody else; and, at last, she disguised this saying as an anecdote and repeated it pleasantly to her husband.

He received it coldly, pondered it with disfavour, and dismissed it by arguing that her Aunt had whiskers, that a whiskered female is a freak, and that the intellectual exercises of a freak are—He lifted his eyebrows and his shoulders. He brushed her Aunt from the tips of his fingers and blew her delicately beyond good manners and the mode.

But time began to hang heavily on both. The intellectual antics of a leisured man become at last wearisome; his methods of thought, by mere familiarity, grow distasteful; the time comes when all the arguments are finished, there is nothing more to be said on any subject, and boredom, without even the covering, apologetic hand, yawns and yawns and cannot be appeased. Thereupon two cease to be company, and even a serpent would be greeted as a cheery and timely visitor. Dismal indeed, and not infrequent, is that time, and the vista therefrom is a long, dull yawn stretching to the horizon and the grave. If at any time we do revalue the values, let us write it down that the person who makes us yawn is a criminal knave, and then we will abolish matrimony and read Plato again.

The serpent arrived one morning hard on Mrs. Morrissy's pathetic pressure. It had three large trunks, a toy terrier, and a volume of verse. The trunks contained dresses, the dog insects, and the book emotion—a sufficiently enlivening trilogy! Miss Sarah O'Malley wore the dresses in exuberant rotation, Mr. Morrissy read the emotional poetry with great admiration, Mrs. Morrissy made friends with the dog, and life at once became complex and joyful.

Mr. Morrissy, exhilarated by the emotional poetry, drew, with an instinct too human to be censured, more and more in the direction of his wife's cousin, and that lady, having a liking for comedy, observed the agile posturings of the gentleman on a verbal summit up and down and around which he flung himself with equal dexterity and satisfaction—crudely, he made puns—and the two were further thrown together by the enforced absences of Mrs. Morrissy, into a privacy more than sealed, by reason of the attentions of a dog who would climb to her lap, and there, with an angry nose, put to no more than temporary rout the nimble guests of his jacket. Shortly Mrs. Morrissy began to look upon the toy terrier with a meditative eye.

It was from one of these, now periodical, retreats that Mrs. Morrissy first observed the rapt attitude of her husband, and, instantly, life for her became bounding, plentiful, and engrossing.

There is no satisfaction in owning that which nobody else covets. Our silver is no more than second-hand, tarnished metal until some one else speaks of it in terms of envy. Our husbands are barely tolerable until a lady friend has endeavoured to abstract their cloying attentions. Then only do we comprehend that our possessions are unique, beautiful, well

James Stephens

worth guarding.

Nobody has yet pointed out that there is an eighth sense; and yet the sense of property is more valuable and more detestable than all the others in combination. The person who owns something is civilised. It is man's escape from wolf and monkeydom. It is individuality at last, or the promise of it, while those other ownerless people must remain either beasts of prey or beasts of burden, grinning with ineffective teeth, or bowing stupid heads for their masters' loads, and all begging humbly for last straws and getting them.

Under a sufficiently equable exterior Mrs. Morrissy's blood was pulsing with greater activity than had ever moved it before. It raced! It flew! At times the tide of it thudded to her head, boomed in her ears, surged in fierce waves against her eyes. Her brain moved with a complexity which would have surprised her had she been capable of remarking upon it. Plot and counterplot! She wove webs horrid as a spider's. She became, without knowing it, a mistress of psychology. She dissected motions and motives. She builded theories precariously upon an eyelash. She pondered and weighed the turning of a head, the handing of a sugar-bowl. She read treason in a laugh, assignations in a song, villainy in a new dress. Deeper and darker things! Profound and vicious depths plunging stark to where the devil lodged in darknesses too dusky for registration! She looked so steadily on these gulfs and murks that at last she could see anything she wished to see; and always, when times were critical, when this and that, abominations indescribable, were separate by no more than a pin's point, she must retire from her watch (alas for a too-sensitive nature!) to chase the enemies of a dog upon which, more than ever, she fixed a meditative eye.

To get that woman out of the house became a pressing necessity. Her cousin carried with her a baleful atmosphere. She moved cloudy with doubt. There was a diabolic aura about her face, and her hair was red! These things were patent. Was one blind or a fool? A straw will reveal the wind, so will an eyelash, a smile, the carriage of a dress. Ankles also! One saw too much of them. Let it be said then. Teeth and neck were bared too often and too broadly. If modesty was indeed more than a name, then here it was outraged. Shame too! was it only a word? Does one do this and that without even a blush? Even vice should have its good manners, its own decent retirements. If there is nothing else let there be breeding! But at this thing the world might look and understand and censure if it were not brass-browed and stupid. Sneak! Traitress! Serpent! Oh, Serpent! do you slip into our very Eden? looping your sly coils across our flowers, trailing over our beds of narcissus and our budding rose, crawling into our secret arbours and whispering-places and nests of happiness! Do you flaunt and sway your crested head with a new hat on it every day? Oh, that my Aunt were here, with the dragon's teeth, and the red breath, and whiskers to match! Here Mrs. Morrissy jumped as if she had been bitten (as indeed she had been) and retired precipitately, eyeing the small dog that frisked about her with an eye almost petrified with meditation.

To get that woman out of the house quickly and without scandal. Not to let her know for a moment, for the blink and twitter of an eyelid, of her triumph. To eject her with ignominy, retaining one's own dignity in the meantime. Never to let her dream of an uneasiness that might have screamed, an anger that could have bitten and scratched and been happy in the primitive exercise. Was such a task beyond her adequacy?

Below in the garden the late sun slanted upon her husband, as with declamatory hands and intense brows he chanted emotional poetry, ready himself on the slope of opportunity to roll into verses from his own resources. He criticised, with agile misconception, the inner meaning, the involved, hard-hidden heart of the poet; and the serpent sat before him and nodded. She smiled enchantments at him, and allurements, and subtle, subtle disagreements. On the grass at their feet the toy terrier bounded from his slumbers and curved an imperative and furious hind-leg in the direction of his ear.

Mrs. Morrissy called the dog, and it followed her into the house, frisking joyously. From the kitchen she procured a small basket, and into this she packed some old cloths and pieces of biscuit. Then she picked up the terrier, cuffed it on both sides of the head, popped it into the basket, tucked its humbly-agitated tail under its abject ribs, closed the basket, and fastened it with a skewer. She next addressed a label to her cousin's home, tied it to the basket, and despatched a servant with it to the railway-station, instructing her that it should be paid for on delivery.

At breakfast the following morning her cousin wondered audibly why her little, weeny, tiny pet was not coming for its brecky.

Mrs. Morrissy, with a smile of infinite sweetness, suggested that Miss O'Malley's father would surely feed the brute when it arrived. "It was a filthy little beast," said she brightly; and she pushed the toast-rack closer to her husband.

There followed a silence which drowsed and buzzed to eternity, and during which Mr. Morrissy's curled moustaches straightened and grew limp and drooped. An edge of ice stiffened around Miss O'Malley. Incredulity, frozen and wan, thawed into swift comprehension and dismay, lit a flame in her cheeks, throbbed burningly at the lobes of her ears, spread magnetic and prickling over her whole stung body, and ebbed and froze again to immobility. She opposed her cousin's kind eyes with a stony brow.

"I think," said she rising, "that I had better see to my packing."

"Must you go?" said Mrs. Morrissy, with courteous unconcern, and she helped herself to cream. Her husband glared insanely at a pat of butter, and tried to look like some one who was somewhere else.

Miss O'Malley closed the door behind her with extreme gentleness.

So the matter lay. But the position was unchanged. For a little time peace would reign in that household, but the same driving necessity remained, and before long another, and perhaps more virulent, serpent would have to be requisitioned for the assuagement of those urgent woes. A man's moustaches will arise with the sun; not Joshua could constrain them to the pillow after the lark had sung reveille. A woman will sit pitilessly at the breakfast table however the male eye may shift and quail. It is the business and the art of life to degrade permanencies. Fluidity is existence, there is no other, and for ever the chief attraction of Paradise must be that there is a serpent in it to keep it lively and wholesome. Lacking the serpent we are no longer in Paradise, we are at home, and our sole entertainment is to yawn when we wish to.

James Stephens

THE DAISIES

In the scented bud of the morning—O,
When the windy grass went rippling far,
I saw my dear one walking slow
In the field where the daisies are.

We did not laugh and we did not speak
As we wandered happily to and fro;
I kissed my dear on either cheek
In the bud of the morning—O.

A lark sang up from the breezy land,
A lark sang down from a cloud afar,
And she and I went hand in hand
In the field where the daisies are.

THREE ANGRY PEOPLE

I

He sat cross-legged on the roadside beside a heap of stones, and with slow regularity his hammer swung up and down, cracking a stone into small pieces at each descent. But his heart was not in the work. He hit whatever stone chanced to be nearest. There was no cunning selection in his hammer, nor any of these oddities of stroke which a curious and interested worker would have essayed for the mere trial of his artistry.

He was not difficult to become acquainted with, and, after a little conversation, I discovered that all the sorrows of the world were sagging from his shoulders. Everything he had ever done was wrong, he said. Everything that people had done to him was wrong, that he affirmed; nor had he any hope that matters would mend, for life was poisoned at the fountain-head and there was no justice anywhere. Justice! he raised his eyebrows with the horrid stare of a man who searches for apparitions; he lowered them again to the bored blink of one who will not believe in apparitions even though he see them—there was not even fairness! Perhaps (and his bearing was mildly tolerant), perhaps some people believed there was fairness, but he had his share of days to count by and remember. Forty-nine years of here and there, and in and out, and up and down; walking all kinds of roads in all kinds of weathers; meeting this sort of person and that sort, and many an adventure that came and passed away without any good to it—"and now," said he sternly, "I am breaking stones on a bye-way."

"A bye-road such as this," said I, "has very few travellers, and it may prove a happy enough retreat."

"Or a hiding-place," said he gloomily.

We sat quietly for a few moments—

"Is there no way of being happy?" said I.

"How could you be happy if you have not got what you want?" and he thumped solidly with his hammer.

"What do you want?" I asked.

"Many a thing," said he, "many a thing."

I squatted on the ground in front of him, and he continued—

"You that are always travelling, did you ever meet a contented person in all your travels?"

"Yes," said I, "I met a man yesterday, three hills away from here, and he told me he was happy."

"Maybe he wasn't a poor man?"

"I asked him that, and he said he had enough to be going on with."

"I wonder what he had."

"I wondered too, and he told me.—He said that he had a wife, a son, an apple-tree, and a fiddle.

"He said, that his wife was dumb, his son was deaf, his apple-tree was barren, and his fiddle was broken."

"It didn't take a lot to satisfy that man."

"And he said, that these things, being the way they were, gave him no trouble attending on them, and so he was left with plenty of time for himself."

"I think the man you are telling me about was a joker; maybe you are a joker yourself for that matter."

"Tell me," said I, "the sort of things a person should want, for I am a young man, and everything one learns is so much to the good."

He rested his hammer and stared sideways down the road, and he remained so, pursing and relaxing his lips, for a little while. At last he said in a low voice—

"A person wants respect from other people.—If he doesn't get that, what does he signify more than a goat or a badger? We live by what folk think of us, and if they speak badly of a man doesn't that finish him for ever?"

"Do people speak well of you?" I asked.

"They speak badly of me," said he, "and the way I am now is this, that I wouldn't have them say a good word of me at all."

"Would you tell me why the people speak badly of you?"

"You are travelling down the road," said he, "and I am staying where I am. We never met before in all the years, and we may never meet again, and so I'll tell you what is in my mind.—A person that has neighbours will have either friends or enemies, and it's likely enough that he'll have the last unless he has a meek spirit. And it's the same way with a man that's married, or a man that has a brother. For the neighbours will spy on you from dawn to dark, and talk about you in every place, and a wife will try to rule you in the house and out of the house until you are badgered to a skeleton, and a brother will ask you to give him whatever thing you value most in the world."

He remained silent for a few minutes, with his hammer eased on his knee, and then, in a more heated strain, he continued—

"These are three things a man doesn't like—he doesn't like to be spied on, and he doesn't like to be ruled and regulated, and he doesn't like to be asked for a thing he wants himself. And, whether he lets himself be spied on or not, he'll be talked about, and in any case he'll be made out to be a queer man; and if he lets his wife rule him he'll be scorned and laughed at, and if he doesn't let her rule him he'll be called a rough man; and if he once gives to his brother he will have to keep on giving for ever, and if he doesn't give in at all he'll get the bad name and the sour look as he goes about his business."

"You have bad neighbours, indeed," said I.

"I'd call them that."

"And a brother that would ask you for a thing you wanted yourself wouldn't be a decent man."

"He would not."

"Tell me," said I, "what kind of a wife have you?"

"She's the same as any one else's wife to look at, but I fancy the other women must be different to live with."

"Why do you say that?"

"Because you can hear men laughing and singing in every public-house that you'd go into, and they wouldn't do that if their wives were hard to live with, for nobody could stand a bad comrade. A good wife, a good brother, a good neighbour—these are three good things, but you don't find them lying in every ditch."

"If you went to a ditch for your wife—!" said I.

He pursed up his lips at me.

"I think," said I, "that you need not mind the neighbours so very much for no one can spy on you but yourself. If your mind was in a glass case instead of in a head it would be different; and no one can really rule and regulate you but yourself, and that's well worth doing."

"Different people," said he shortly, "are made differently."

"Maybe," said I, "your wife would be a good wife to some other husband, and your brother might be decent enough if he had a different brother."

He wrinkled up his eyes and looked at me very steadily—

"I'll be saying good-bye to you, young man," said he, and he raised his hammer again and began to beat solemnly on the stones.

I stood by him for a few minutes, but as he neither spoke nor looked at me again I turned to my own path intending to strike Dublin by the Paps of Dana and the long slopes beyond them.

II

One day he chucked his job, put up his tools, told the boss he could do this and that, called hurroo to the boys, and sauntered out of the place with a great deal of dignity and one week's wages in cash.

There were many reasons why he should not have quitted his work, not the lightest of them being that the food of a wife and family depended on his sticking to it, but a person who has a temper cannot be expected to have everything else.

Nothing makes a man feel better than telling his employer that he and his job can go bark at one another. It is the dream of a great many people, and were it not for the glamour of that idea most folk would commit suicide through sheer disgust. Getting the "sack" is an experience which wearies after the first time. Giving the sack is a felicity granted only to a few people. To go home to one's wife with the information that you have been discharged is an adventure which one does not wish to repeat, but to go home and hand her thirty shillings with the statement that you have discharged yourself is not one of the pleasantest ways of passing time.

His wife's habits were as uncertain as her temper, but not as bad. She had a hot tongue, a red head, a quick fist and a big family—ingredients to compose a peppery dish. They had been only a short time married when she gave her husband to understand that there was to be only one head of that household, and that would not be he. He fought fiercely for a position on the executive but he did not get it. His voice in the household economy, which had commenced with the lordly "Let this be done," concluded in the timidly blustering "All right, have it your own way."

Furthermore, the theory that a woman is helpmate to a man was repugnant to her. She believed and asserted that a man had to be managed, and she had several maxims to which she often gave forcible and contemptuous utterance—

"Let a man go his own road to-day and he will be shaking hands with the devil to-morrow.

"Give a man his head and he'll lose it.

"Whiskers and sense were never found in the same patch.

"There's more brains in one woman's finger than there is in the congregated craniums of a battalion of men folk.

"Where there is two men there's one fight. Where there's three there's a drinking match, two fights and a fine to be paid."

But while advocating peace at any price and a tax on muscles that were bigger than a fly's knuckle she was herself a warrior of the breed of Finn and strong enough to scare a pugilist. When she was angry her family got over the garden wall, her husband first. She did not think very much of him, and she told him so, but he was sufficient of a man not to believe her.

For a long time he had been a dissatisfied person, leading a grumpy existence which was only made bearable by gusts of solitary blasphemy. When a man curses openly he is healthy enough, but when he takes to either swearing or drinking in secret then he has travelled almost beyond redemption point.

So behold our man knocking at the door, still warmed by the fray with his late employer, but with the first tremors of fear beginning to tatter up and down his spine.

His wife opened the door herself. She was engaged in cleaning the place, a duty in which she was by no means remiss, one of the prime points in her philosophy being that a house was not clean until one's food could be eaten off the floor. She was a big comely woman, but at the moment she did not look dainty. A long wisp of red hair came looping down on her shoulders. A smear of soot toned down the roses of her cheek, her arms were smothered in soap suds, and the fact that she was wearing a pair of her husband's boots added nothing to her attractions.

When she saw her husband standing in the doorway at this unaccustomed hour she was a little taken aback, but, scenting trouble, she at once opened the attack—

"What in the name of heaven brings you here at this hour of the day, and the place upset the way it is? Don't walk on the soap, man, haven't you got eyes in your head?"

"I'm not walking on the soap with my head," he retorted, "if I was I'd see it, and if it wasn't on the floor it wouldn't be tripping folk up. A nice thing it is that a man can't come into his own house without being set slipping and sliding like an acrobat on an iceberg."

"And," cried his wife, "if I kept the soap locked up it's the nice, clean house you'd have to come into. Not that you'd mind if the place was dirty, I'll say that much for you, for what one is reared to one likes, and what is natural is pleasant. But I got a different rearing let me tell you, and while I'm in it I'll have the clean house no matter who wants the dirty one."

"You will so," said he, looking at the soapy water for a place to walk on.

"Can't you be coming in then, and not stand there framed in the doorway, gawking like a fool at a miracle."

"I'll sail across if you'll get a canal boat or a raft," said he, "or, if the children are kept out of sight, I'll strip, ma'm, and swim for it."

His wife regarded him with steady gloom.

"If you took the smallest interest in your home," said she, "and were less set on gallivanting about the country, going to the

Lord knows where, with the Lord knows who, you'd know that the children were away in school at this hour. Nice indeed the places you visit and the company you keep, if the truth were known—walk across it, man, and wipe your feet on the kitchen mat."

So he walked into the kitchen, and sat down, and, as he sat, the last remnants of his courage trembled down into his boots and evaporated.

His wife came in after him—she drooped a speculative eye on her lord—

"You didn't say what brought you home so early," said she.

When a hard thing has to be done the quickest way is generally the best way. It is like the morning bath—don't ruminate, jump in, for the longer you wait the more dubious you get, and the tub begins to look arctic and repellent.

Some such philosophy as this dictated his attitude. He lugged out his week's wages, slapped it on the table, and said—

"I've got the sack."

Then he stretched his legs out, pushed his fists deep into his trouser pockets, and waited.

His wife sat down too, slowly and with great care, and she stared in silence at her husband—

"Do you tell me you have lost your employment?" said she in a quiet voice.

"I do, then," said he. "I chucked it myself. I told old Whiskers that he could go and boil his job and his head together and sell the soup for cat-lap."

"You threw up your situation yourself."

"You've got the truth of it, ma'm," he rejoined.

"Maybe you'd be telling me what you did the like of that for?"

"Because," said he, "I'm a man and not a mouse. Because I don't want to be at the beck and call of every dog and devil that has a bit more money than I have—a man has got to be a man sometimes," he growled.

"Sure, you're telling the truth," said his wife, nodding her head at him. "A man should be a man sometimes. It's the pity of the world that he can't be a man always: and, indeed, it's the hard thing for a woman to tell herself that the man she has got isn't a man at all, but a big fool with no more wit than a boy."

Now this was the first time he had found his wife take trouble lying down. As a rule she was readier for a fight than he was. She jumped into a row with the alacrity of a dog: and the change worked on him. He looked at her listless hands, and the sight of those powerful organs hanging so powerlessly wrought on him. Women often forget that their weakness is really their strength. The weakest things in the world are by a queer paradox always the strongest. The toughest stone will ear away under the dropping of water, a mushroom will lift a rock on its delicate head, a child will make its father work for it. So the too capable woman will always have a baby to nurse, and that baby will be her husband. If she buttress her womanhood too much she saps his manhood. Let her love all she can and never stint that blessing, but a woman cannot often be obeyed and loved at the same time. A man cannot obey a woman constantly and retain his self-respect: the muscles of his arms reproach him if he does, and the man with his self-respect gone is a man with a grudge, he will learn to hate the agent who brought him low. A day may come when he will rise and beat her in self-defence, with his fists if he is sufficiently brutalised, some subtler, but no less efficient, weapon if his manhood refuses to be degraded—and this was our case. His wife had grabbed the reins and driven the matrimonial coach: driven it well, that is true, but the driver, by right of precedent, had sat by hurt and angry, and at last, in an endeavour to prove his manhood among men, he had damned his employer's self and work, although in reality all his fury was directed against the mother of his children. He threw up his work, and the semi-conscious thought that went home with him was—"Now she will be sorry. If she must do everything let her earn the bread."

The woman knew what poverty meant, and she had four young children. It was the thought of these helpless ones crying with hunger (she could hear them already, her ears were dinned with their hungry lamentation) that took the fibre out of her arms, and left her without any fight. She could only sit and look with wretched eyes on the man whom she had been demoralising, and, for the first time since he knew her, the tears came, and the poor woman laid her head on the kitchen table and wept.

He was astonished, he was dismayed, but he could not stand her tears: he ran to her—the first time he ever did run to her—

"Sure, darling," said he, "is it crying you are? What would you be doing that for? If I've lost one job I can get another. I'm not afraid of work, and I know how to do it. I'll get something to do at once, if it's only wheeling a handcart, or selling cockles in public-houses. Wisha, dry your eyes—they're as pretty as they ever were," said he, trying to look at them, while his wife, with a strange shyness, would not let him see, for she felt that there was a strange man with her, some one she did not know. That was a man's hand on her shoulder, and she had never felt a man's hand before, as long as she was married.

"I'll go out at once," said he, "and when I come in to-night I'll have a job if I have to bang it out of some one with a shovel."

He slapped on his hat, kicked the soap out of the way, tramped through the water on the floor, and when at the door he turned again and came back to kiss his wife, a form of caress which had long fallen into desuetude, and so, out into the street, a man again.

James Stephens

When he had gone his wife returned to her scrubbing, and, as she worked she smiled at something she was remembering, and, now and again, a bit of a song came from lips that had scolded so much. Having finished her work she spent nearly an hour at the looking-glass doing up her hair (grand hair it was, too) with her ears listening for a footstep. Now and again she would run to the pot to see were the potatoes doing all right— "The children will be in shortly," said she, "and hungry to the bone, poor dears."

But she was not thinking of the children. The warmth of a kiss was still on her lips. Something in the back of her head was saying—"He will do it again when he comes in."

And the second honeymoon was pleasanter than the first.

III

She was tall and angular. Her hair was red, and scarce, and untidy. Her hands were large and packed all over with knuckles and her feet would have turned inwards at the toes, only that she was aware of and corrected their perversities.

She was sitting all alone, and did not look up as I approached—

"Tell me," said I, "why you have sat for more than an hour with your eyes fixed on nothing, and your hands punching your lap?"

She looked at me for a fleeting instant, and then, looking away again, she began to speak.—Her voice was pleasant enough, but it was so strong that one fancied there were bones in it—

"I do not dislike women," said she, "but I think they seldom speak of anything worth listening to, nor do they often do anything worth looking at: they bore and depress me, and men do not."

"But," said I, "you have not explained why you thump your lap with your fist?"

She proceeded—

"I do not hate women, nor do I love men. It was only that I did not take much notice of the one, and that I liked being with the other, for, as things are, there is very little life for a person except in thinking. All our actions are so cumbered by laws and customs that we cannot take a step beyond the ordinary without finding ourselves either in gaol or in Coventry."

Having said this, she raised her bleak head and stared like an eagle across the wastes.

After I had coughed twice I touched her arm, and said—

"Yes?"

"One must live," said she quickly. "I do not mean that we must eat and sleep—these mechanical matters are settled for many of us, but life consists in thinking, and nothing else, yet many people go from the cradle to the grave without having lived differently from animals. I do not want to be one of them. Their whole theory of life is mechanical. They eat and drink. They invite each other to their houses to eat and drink, and they use such speech as they are gifted with in discussing their food and whatever other palpable occurrence may have chanced to them in the day. It is a step, perhaps, towards living, but it is still only one step removed from stagnation. They have some interest in an occurrence, but how that occurrence happened, and what will result from it does not exercise them in the least, and these, which are knowledge and prophecy, are the only interesting aspects of any event."

"But," said I, "you have not told me why you sit for a full hour staring at vacancy, and thumping on your knee with your hand?"

She continued—.

"Sometimes one meets certain people who have sufficient of the divine ferment in their heads to be called alive: they are almost always men. We fly to them as to our own people. We abase ourselves before them in happy humility. We crave to be allowed to live near them in order that we may be assured that everything in the world is not nonsense and machinery—and then, what do we find—?"

She paused, and turned a large fierce eye upon me.

"I do not know," said I, and I endeavoured vainly to look everywhere but at her eye.

"We find always that they are married," said she, and, saying so, she lapsed again to a tense and worried reflection.

"You have not told me," I insisted gently, "why you peer earnestly into space, and thump at intervals upon your knee with the heel of your fist?"

"These men," said she sternly, "are surrounded by their wives. They are in gaol and their wives are their warders. You cannot go to them without a permit. You may not speak to them without a listener. You may not argue with them for fear of raising an alien and ridiculous hostility. Scarcely can you even look at them without reproach.—How then can we live, and how will the torch of life be kept alight?"

"I do not know," I murmured.

She turned her pale eye to me again.

"I am not beautiful," said she.

But there was just a tremor of doubt in her voice, so that the apparent statement became packed with curiosity, and had all the quality of a question.

I did not shrug my shoulder nor raise an eyebrow—

"You are very nice," I replied.

"I do not want to be beautiful," she continued severely. "Why should I? I have no interest in such things. I am interested only in living, and living is thinking; but I demand access to my fellows who are alive. Perhaps, I did not pay those others enough attention. How could I? They cannot think. They cannot speak. They make a complicated verbal noise, but all I am able to translate from it is, that a something called lip-salve can be bought in some particular shop one penny cheaper than it can in a certain other shop. They will twitter for hours about the way a piece of ribbon was stitched to a hat which they saw

James Stephens

in a tramcar. They agitate themselves wondering whether a muff should be this size or that size?—I say, they depress me, and if I do turn my back on them when men are present I am only acting sensibly and justly. Why cannot they twitter to each other and let me and other people alone?"

She turned to me again—

"I do not know," said I meekly.

"And," she continued, "the power they have; the amazing power they have to annoy other folk. All kinds of sly impertinences, vulgar evasions, and sneering misunderstandings. Why should such women be allowed to take men into their captivity, to sequester, and gag, and restrain them from those whom they would naturally be eager to meet?

"What," she continued fiercely, "had my hat to do with that woman, or my frock?"

I nodded slowly and grievously, and repeated—

"What indeed?"

"A hat," said she, "is something to cover one's head from the rain, and a frock is something to guard one's limbs from inclement weather.—To that extent I am interested in these things: but they would put a hat on my mind, and a black cloth on my understanding."

We sat in silence for a little time, while she surveyed the bleak horizon as an eagle might.

"And when I call at their houses," said she, "their servants say 'Not at home,' a lie, you know, and they close their doors on me."

She was silent again—

"I do not know what to do," said she.

"Is that," said I, "the reason why you beat your lap with your hand, and stare abroad like a famished eagle?"

She turned quickly to me—

"What shall I do to open those doors?" said she.

"If I happened to be you," I replied, "I would cut off my hair, I'd buy a man's clothes and wear them always, I'd call myself Harry or Tom; and then I'd go wherever I pleased, and meet whoever I wanted to meet?"

She stared fixedly at herself in these garments, and under these denominations—

"They would know I was not a man," said she gravely.

I looked at her figure—

"No person in the world would ever guess it," said I.

She arose from her seat. She clutched her reticule to her breast—

"I'll do it," said she, and she stalked gauntly across the fields.

James Stephens

THE THREEPENNY-PIECE

When Brien O'Brien died, people said that it did not matter very much, because he would have died young in any case. He would have been hanged, or his head would have been split in two halves with a hatchet, or he would have tumbled down the cliff when he was drunk and been smashed into jelly. Something like that was due to him, and everybody likes to see a man get what he deserves to get.

But, as ethical writs cease to run when a man is dead, the neighbours did not stay away from his wake. They came, and they said many mitigating things across the body with the bandaged jaws and the sly grin, and they reminded each other of this and that queer thing which he had done, for his memory was crusted over with stories of wild, laughable things, and other things which were wild but not laughable.

Meanwhile, he was dead, and one was at liberty to be a trifle sorry for him. Further, he belonged to the O'Brien nation, a stock to whom reverence was due. A stock not easily forgotten. The historic memory could reconstruct forgotten glories of station and battle, of terrible villainy and terrible saintliness, the pitiful, valorous, slow descent to the degradation which was not yet wholly victorious. A great stock! The O'Neills remembered it. The O'Tools and the MacSweeneys had stories by the hundred of love and hate. The Burkes and the Geraldines and the new strangers had memories also.

His family was left in the poorest way, but they were used to that, for he had kept them as poor as he left them, or found them, for that matter. They had shaken hands with Charity so often that they no longer disliked the sallow-faced lady, and, so, certain small gifts made by the neighbours were accepted, not very thankfully, but very readily. These gifts were almost always in kind. A few eggs. A bag of potatoes. A handful of meal. A couple of twists of tea—such like.

One of the visitors, however, moved by an extraordinary dejection, slipped a silver threepenny-piece into the hand of Brien's little daughter, Sheila, aged four years, and later on she did not like to ask for it back again.

Little Sheila had been well trained by her father. She knew exactly what should be done with money, and so, when nobody was looking, she tip-toed to the coffin and slipped the threepenny-piece into Brien's hand. That hand had never refused money when it was alive, it did not reject it either when it was dead.

They buried him the next day.

He was called up for judgment the day after, and made his appearance with a miscellaneous crowd of wretches, and there he again received what was due to him. He was removed protesting and struggling to the place decreed.

"Down," said Rhadamanthus, pointing with his great hand, and down he went.

In the struggle he dropped the threepenny-piece, but he was so bustled and heated that he did not observe his loss. He went down, far down, out of sight, out of remembrance, to a howling, black gulf with others of his unseen kind.

A young seraph, named Cuchulain, chancing to pass that way shortly afterwards, saw the threepenny-piece peeping brightly from the rocks, and he picked it up.

James Stephens

He looked at it in astonishment. He turned it over and over, this way and that way. Examined it at the stretch of his arm, and peered minutely at it from two inches distance—

"I have never in my life seen anything so beautifully wrought," said he, and, having stowed it in his pouch along with some other trinkets, he strolled homewards again through the massy gates.

It was not long until Brien discovered his loss, and, suddenly, through the black region, his voice went mounting and brawling.

"I have been robbed," he yelled. "I have been robbed in heaven!"

Having begun to yell he did not stop. Sometimes he was simply angry and made a noise. Sometimes he became sarcastic and would send his query swirling upwards—

"Who stole the threepenny-bit?" he roared. He addressed the surrounding black space—

"Who stole the last threepenny-bit of a poor man?"

Again and again his voice pealed upwards. The pains of his habitation lost all their sting for him. His mind had nourishment and the heat within him vanquished the fumes without. He had a grievance, a righteous cause, he was buoyed and strengthened, nothing could silence him. They tried ingenious devices, all kinds of complicated things, but he paid no heed, and the tormentors were in despair.

"I hate these sinners from the kingdom of Kerry," said the Chief Tormentor, and he sat moodily down on his own circular saw; and that worried him also, for he was clad only in a loin cloth.

"I hate the entire Clan of the Gael," said he; "why cannot they send them somewhere else?" and then he started practising again on Brien.

It was no use. Brien's query still blared upwards like the sound of the great trump itself. It wakened and rung the rocky caverns, screamed through fissure and funnel, and was battered and slung from pinnacle to crag and up again. Worse! his companions in doom became interested and took up the cry, until at last the uproar became so appalling that the Master himself could not stand it.

"I have not had a wink of sleep for three nights," said that harassed one, and he sent a special embassy to the powers.

Rhadamanthus was astonished when they arrived. His elbow was leaning on his vast knee, and his heavy head rested on a hand that was acres long, acres wide.

"What is all this about?" said he.

"The Master cannot go to sleep," said the spokesman of the embassy, and he grinned as he said it, for it sounded queer even to himself.

"It is not necessary that he should sleep," said Rhadamanthus. "I have never slept since time began, and I will never sleep until time is over. But the complaint is curious. What has troubled your master?"

"Hell is turned upside down and inside out," said the fiend. "The tormentors are weeping like little children. The principalities are squatting on their hunkers doing nothing. The orders are running here and there fighting each other. The styles are leaning against walls shrugging their shoulders, and the damned are shouting and laughing and have become callous to torment."

"It is not my business," said the judge.

"The sinners demand justice," said the spokesman.

"They've got it," said Rhadamanthus, "let them stew in it."

"They refuse to stew," replied the spokesman, wringing his hands.

Rhadamanthus sat up.

"It is an axiom in law," said he, "that however complicated an event may be, there can never be more than one person at the extreme bottom of it. Who is the person?"

"It is one Brien of the O'Brien nation, late of the kingdom of Kerry. A bad one! He got the maximum punishment a week ago."

For the first time in his life Rhadamanthus was disturbed. He scratched his head, and it was the first time he had ever done that either.

"You say he got the maximum," said Rhadamanthus, "then it's a fix! I have damned him for ever, and better or worse than that cannot be done. It is none of my business," said he angrily, and he had the deputation removed by force.

But that did not ease the trouble. The contagion spread until ten million billions of voices were chanting in unison, and uncountable multitudes were listening between their pangs.

"Who stole the threepenny-bit? Who stole the threepenny-bit?"

That was still their cry. Heaven rang with it as well as hell. Space was filled with that rhythmic tumult. Chaos and empty Nox had a new discord added to their elemental throes. Another memorial was drafted below, showing that unless the missing coin was restored to its owner hell would have to close its doors. There was a veiled menace in the memorial also, for

Clause 6 hinted that if hell was allowed to go by the board heaven might find itself in some jeopardy thereafter.

The document was dispatched and considered. In consequence a proclamation was sent through all the wards of Paradise, calling on whatever person, archangel, seraph, cherub, or acolyte had found a threepenny-piece since midday of the tenth of August then instant, that the same person, archangel, seraph, cherub, or acolyte, should deliver the said threepenny-piece to Rhadamanthus at his Court, and should receive in return a free pardon and a receipt.

The coin was not delivered,

That young seraph, Cuchulain, walked about like a person who was strange to himself. He was not tormented: he was angry. He frowned, he cogitated and fumed. He drew one golden curl through his fingers until it was lank and drooping; save the end only, that was still a ripple of gold. He put the end in his mouth and strode moodily chewing it. And every day his feet turned in the same direction—down the long entrance boulevard, through the mighty gates, along the strip of carved slabs, to that piled wilderness where Rhadamanthus sat monumentally.

Here delicately he went, sometimes with a hand outstretched to help his foothold, standing for a space to think ere he jumped to a further rock, balancing himself for a moment ere he leaped again. So he would come to stand and stare gloomily upon the judge.

He would salute gravely, as was meet, and say, "God bless the work"; but Rhadamanthus never replied, save by a nod, for he was very busy.

Yet the judge did observe him, and would sometimes heave ponderous lids to where he stood, and so, for a few seconds, they regarded each other in an interval of that unceasing business.

James Stephens

Sometimes for a minute or two the young seraph Cuchulain would look from the judge to the judged as they crouched back or strained forward, the good and the bad all in the same tremble of fear, all unknowing which way their doom might lead. They did not look at each other. They looked at the judge high on his ebon throne, and they could not look away from him. There were those who knew, guessed clearly their doom; abashed and flaccid they sat, quaking. There were some who were uncertain—rabbit-eyed these, not less quaking than the others, biting at their knuckles as they peeped upwards. There were those hopeful, yet searching fearfully backwards in the wilderness of memory, chasing and weighing their sins; and these last, even when their bliss was sealed and their steps set on an easy path, went faltering, not daring to look around again, their ears strained to catch a—"Halt, miscreant! this other is your way!"

So, day by day, he went to stand near the judge; and one day Rhadamanthus, looking on him more intently, lifted his great hand and pointed—

"Go you among those to be judged," said he.

For Rhadamanthus knew. It was his business to look deep into the heart and the mind, to fish for secrets in the pools of being.

And the young seraph Cuchulain, still rolling his golden curl between his lips, went obediently forward and set down his nodding plumes between two who whimpered and stared and quaked.

When his turn came, Rhadamanthus eyed him intently for a long time—

"Well!" said Rhadamanthus.

The young seraph Cuchulain blew the curl of gold away from his mouth—

"Findings are keepings," said he loudly, and he closed his mouth and stared very impertinently at the judge.

"It is to be given up," said the judge.

"Let them come and take it from me," said the seraph Cuchulain. And suddenly (for these things are at the will of spirits) around his head the lightnings span, and his hands were on the necks of thunders.

For the second time in his life Rhadamanthus was disturbed, again he scratched his head—

"It's a fix," said he moodily. But in a moment he called to those whose duty it was—

"Take him to this side," he roared.

And they advanced. But the seraph Cuchulain swung to meet them, and his golden hair blazed and shrieked; and the thunders rolled at his feet, and about him a bright network that hissed and stung—and those who advanced turned haltingly backwards and ran screaming.

"It's a fix," said Rhadamanthus; and for a little time he stared menacingly at the seraph Cuchulain.

But only for a little time. Suddenly he put his hands on the rests of his throne and heaved upwards his terrific bulk. Never before had Rhadamanthus stood from his ordained chair. He strode mightily forward and in an instant had quelled that rebel. The thunders and lightnings were but moonbeams and dew on that stony carcass. He seized the seraph Cuchulain, lifted him to his breast as one lifts a sparrow, and tramped back with him—

"Fetch me that other," said he, sternly, and he sat down.

Those whose duty it was sped swiftly downwards to find Brien of the O'Brien nation; and while they were gone, all in vain the seraph Cuchulain crushed flamy barbs against that bosom of doom. Now, indeed, his golden locks were drooping and his plumes were broken and tossed; but his fierce eye still glared courageously against the nipple of Rhadamanthus.

Soon they brought Brien. He was a sight of woe—howling, naked as a tree in winter, black as a tarred wall, carved and gashed, tattered in all but his throat, wherewith, until one's ears rebelled, he bawled his one demand.

But the sudden light struck him to a wondering silence, and the sight of the judge holding the seraph Cuchulain like a limp flower to his breast held him gaping—

"Bring him here," said Rhadamanthus.

And they brought him to the steps of the throne—

"You have lost a medal!" said Rhadamanthus. "This one has it."

Brien looked straitly at the seraph Cuchulain.

Rhadamanthus stood again, whirled his arm in an enormous arc, jerked, and let go, and the seraph Cuchulain went swirling through space like a slung stone—

"Go after him, Kerryman," said Rhadamanthus, stooping; and he seized Brien by the leg, whirled him wide and out and far; dizzy, dizzy as a swooping comet, and down, and down, and down.

Rhadamanthus seated himself. He motioned with his hand—

"Next," said he, coldly.

Down went the seraph Cuchulain, swirling in wide tumbles, scarcely visible for quickness. Sometimes, with outstretched hands, he was a cross that dropped plumb. Anon, head urgently downwards, he dived steeply. Again, like a living hoop, head and heels together, he spun giddily. Blind, deaf, dumb, breathless, mindless; and behind him Brien of the O'Brien nation came pelting and whizzing.

What of that journey! Who could give it words? Of the suns that appeared and disappeared like winking eyes. Comets that shone for an instant, went black and vanished. Moons that came, and stood, and were gone. And around all, including all, boundless space, boundless silence; the black, unmoving void—the deep, unending quietude, through which they fell with Saturn and Orion, and mildly-smiling Venus, and the fair, stark-naked moon and the decent earth wreathed in pearl and blue. From afar she appeared, the quiet one, all lonely in the void. As sudden as a fair face in a crowded street. Beautiful as the sound of falling waters. Beautiful as the sound of music in a silence. Like a white sail on a windy sea. Like a green tree in a solitary place. Chaste and wonderful she was. Flying afar. Flying aloft like a joyous bird when the morning breaks on the darkness and he shrills sweet tidings. She soared and sang. Gently she sang to timid pipes and flutes of tender straw and murmuring, distant strings. A song that grew and swelled, gathering to a multitudinous, deep-thundered harmony, until the over-burdened ear failed before the appalling uproar of her ecstasy, and denounced her. No longer a star! No longer a bird! A plumed and horned fury! Gigantic, gigantic, leaping and shrieking tempestuously, spouting whirlwinds of lightning, tearing gluttonously along her path, avid, rampant, howling with rage and terror she leaped, dreadfully she leaped and flew. . . .

Enough! They hit the earth—they were not smashed, there was that virtue in them. They hit the ground just outside the village of Donnybrook where the back road runs to the hills; and scarcely had they bumped twice when Brien of the O'Brien nation had the seraph Cuchulain by the throat—

"My threepenny-bit," he roared, with one fist up—

But the seraph Cuchulain only laughed—

"That!" said he. "Look at me, man. Your little medal dropped far beyond the rings of Saturn."

And Brien stood back looking at him—He was as naked as Brien was. He was as naked as a stone, or an eel, or a pot, or a new-born babe. He was very naked.

So Brien of the O'Brien nation strode across the path and sat down by the side of a hedge—

"The first man that passes this way," said he, "will give me his clothes, or I'll strangle him."

The seraph Cuchulain walked over to him—

"I will take the clothes of the second man that passes," said he, and he sat down.

BRIGID

(AFTER THE IRISH)

Do not marry, Breed, asthore!
That old man whose head is hoar
As the winter, but instead
Mate with some young curly-head;
He will give to you a child,
He will never leave your side,
And at morning when you wake
Kiss for kiss will give and take.

I wish that I had died, I do,
Before I gave my love to you;
Love so lasting that it will
While I live be with you still:
And for it what do I get?
Pain and trouble and regret,
The terrors of the aspen-tree
Which the wind shakes fearfully.

If this country could be seen
As it ought—then you had been
Living in a castle grand
With the ladies of the land:
The friend and foe, the gael and gall,
Would be cheering, one and all,
For yourself, and, this is true,
I would be along with you.

James Stephens

You promised, 'twas a lie, I see,
When you said you'd come to me
At the sheep-cote; I was there,
And I whistled on the air,
And I gave our settled call—
But you were not there at all!
There was nothing anywhere
But lambs and birds and sunny air

When it is dark you pass me by,
And when the sun is in the sky
You pass me also—night or day
You look away, you walk away!
But if you would come to me,
And say the word of courtesy,
I would close the door, and then
I'd never let you out again.

But do not marry, Breed, asthore!
That old man; his heart is hoar
As his head is: you can see
Winter gripping at his knee:
His eyes and ears are blear and dim,
How can you expect of him
To see or hear or pleasure you
Half as well as I would do?

THREE YOUNG WIVES

I

She was about to be a mother for the second time, and the fear which is the portion of women was upon her. In a little while she would be in the toils, and she hated and feared physical pain with a great hatred and a great fear. But there was something further which distressed her.

She was a soft, babyish creature, downy and clinging, soft-eyed and gentle, the beggar folk had received gifts at her hand, the dogs knew of her largesse. Men looked on her with approval, and women liked her. Her husband belonged to the type known as "fine men," tall, generously-proportioned, with the free and easy joviality which is so common in Ireland. He was born a boy and he would never grow out of that state. The colour of his hair or the wrinkles on his cheek would not have anything to do with his age, for time was powerless against the richness of his blood. He would still be a boy when he was dying of old age; but if protestations, kisses and homage were any criterion then the fact that he loved his wife was fixed beyond any kind of doubt.

But he did not love her.—He was as changeable as the weather of his country. Swift to love he was equally swift to forget. His passions were of primitive intensity, but they were not steadfast. He clutched with both hands at the present and was surprised and irritated by the fact that he could in nowise get

James Stephens

away from the past: the future he did not care a rap about. Nobody does: there is, indeed, no such thing as the future, there is only the possibility of it, but the past and the present are facts not to be gotten away from. What we have done and what we are doing are things which stamp us, mould us, live with us and after us: what we will do cannot be counted on, has no part in us, has only a problematical existence, and can be interfered with, hindered, nullified or amplified by the thousand unmanageable accidents of futurity.

He had married thanking God from a full heart for His goodness, and believing implicitly that he had plucked the very Flower of Womanhood, and the Heart of the World, and, maybe, he had.—There are many Flowers of Womanhood, all equally fragrant, and the Heart of the World can beat against the breast of any man who loves a woman.

Some time previously their little boy had contracted small-pox, and his mother, nursing him, took it from him. When they recovered her beauty was gone. The extraordinary bloom which had made her cheek a shrine to worship and marvel at was destroyed for ever, while, by a curious chance, the boy was unmarked.

Now the only love which he had to give was a physical love. He did not love a woman, he loved the husk. Of the woman herself he knew nothing and cared less. He had never sought to know his wife, never tried to pierce beneath her beauty and discover where the woman lived and what she was like at home. Indeed, he knew less of his wife than his servants did, and by little and little she had seen how the matter stood. She had plucked the heart from his mystery and read him to the bones, while remaining herself intact. But she held him still, although by the most primitive and fragile of bonds, by the magnetism of her body, the shining of her eyes, the soft beauty of her cheeks; and, behold! she was undone. The disease had stamped on her face, and, in the recoil, had stamped on her husband's love.

How many nights of solitary tears she had known! she alone could count them, a heavy knowledge. How many slights, shrinkings, coldnesses she had discerned! the tale of them was hot in her brain, the index heavy on her heart.

She knew her loss on the day that her husband looked at her after her recovery when all fear of infection had passed—the stare, the flush, the angry disgust. Her eyes were cameras. She had only to close them and she could see again in dismal procession those dismal details.

And now, as she lay helpless on the bed, she watched him. She was racked with pain, and he was mumbling that it would be all right again in a little time. "A week from now," said he, "and you will have forgotten all about it."

But she, looking at him with fearful eyes, traced this sentence at the back of his brain, "I hope that she will die," and the life within her which had been sown in happiness and love, and had grown great through misery and tears was now beating at the gates of entrance. . . . She might die: so many people die in labour, and she was not strong. With a new clairvoyant gaze she saw Death standing by the bed, hooded, cloaked and sombre; his eyes were fixed on her and they were peaceful and kindly eyes. Had there been nothing else to care for she would have gone gladly to the Dark One; but there remained her little son. What heart was he to rest on when she was gone? Whose arms could open so widely as the mother's when he fled from the terrible things which haunt Babyland?—it was an arrow in her heart.

She knew well that her husband would marry again. He was of those men who are inveterate husbands—and that new woman!—Who was she? What was she like? What would be her attitude towards a motherless child? towards her little one? She would be kindly at first, little doubt of that, but afterwards, when her own children came, what would become of the child of a husband's first wife? . . .

She stared down vistas of sorrow. She was a woman, and she knew women. She saw the other little ones, strangers to her, cared for and loved, all their childish troubles the centre of maternal interest and debate, while her boy slunk through a lonely, pathetic childhood, frightened, repressed, perhaps beaten, because he was not of the brood. . . .

She saw these things as she lay looking at her husband, and she believed they would come to pass if she died.

And in the night time, when the stars were hidden behind the window curtains, by the light of a lamp that fell on toiling, anxious people, in a hospital-like atmosphere of pain and clamour she did die.

II

It was believed long ago in the ancient kingdom of Erinn that it was death to be a poet, death to love a poet, and death to mock a poet. So the Gael said, and, in that distant time, the people of the Gael were a wise people, holding the ancient knowledge, and they honoured the poet and feared him, for his fostering was among the people of the Shee, and his curse was quickened with the authority of the gods. Even lately the people feared the poets and did them reverence, although the New Ignorance (known humorously as Education) was gradually strangling the life out of Wisdom, and was setting up a different and debased standard of mental values. There was a lady once and she scorned a poet, wittingly and with malice, and it was ill for her in the sequel, for the gods saw to it.

She was very beautiful—"The finest girl in three counties, sir," said her father: but he might have been prejudiced in favour of his own, and he had been known to speak of himself as "the finest man in Ireland, and you know what that means, sir." Further, his dog was "the greatest dog that ever ratted in the universe." Whatever he owned was not only good, it was great and unique, and whatever he did not own had, in his opinion, very little to recommend it.

But his daughter was beautiful. When the male eye encountered her it was in no haste to look away. When the female eye lit on her it was, and the owner of the female eye, having sniffed as was proper, went home and tried to do up her hair or her complexion in the like manner—as was also proper. A great many people believe (and who will quarrel with their verities) that beauty is largely a matter of craft and adjustment.—Such women are beautiful with a little difficulty—they pursue loveliness, run it to earth in a shop, obtain it with a certain amount of minted metal, and reincarnate themselves from a box.—They deserve all the success which they undoubtedly obtain. There are other women who are beautiful by accident—such as, the cunning disposition of a dimple, the abilities of a certain kind of smile, the possession of a charming voice—for, indeed, an ugly woman with a beautiful voice is a beautiful woman. But some women are beautiful through the spendthrift generosity of nature, and of this last was she. Whatever of colour, line, or motion goes to the construction of beauty that she was heiress to, and she knew it only too well.

A person who has something of his own making may properly be proud of his possession, even if it is nothing more than a stamp album, but a person who has been gifted by Providence or Fairy Godmothers should not be conceited. A self-made man may be proud of his money, but his son may not. Pride in what has been given freely to you is an empty pride, and she was prouder of her beauty than a poet is of his odes—it was her undoing in the end.

She was so accustomed to the homage of men that one who failed to make instant and humble obeisance to her proved himself to be either a very vulgar person or else a miracle. Such folk were few, for the average man bends as readily to beauty as a flower sways to the wind, or the sea to the touch of the moon.

Before she was twenty years of age she had loomed in the eye of every male in her vicinity as the special female whom nature had built to his exclusive measure. When she was twenty-one she had withstood the matrimonial threats of half the male population of Ireland, and she knew how every social grade (there are not many of them) of Irish life made love, for that was the only thing they were able to do while they were near her. From the farmer with a spade in his fist to the landlord with a writ in his agent's pocket, all sang the same song, the sole difference being a matter of grammar; and, although young women have big appetites in these cases, and great recuperative powers, she was as tired of love and love-lorn swains as a young and healthy woman can be, and then, suddenly, and to her own delighted consternation, she did fall in love.

The tantalising part of the whole matter was that she was unable to formulate any good reason for falling in love with this particular male. Her powers of observation (and they were as sharp as a cat's tooth) pointed out that although he was a young man his head was beginning to push out through his hair, and she had always considered that a bald man was outside the pale of human interest. Furthermore, his trousers bagged at the knees, perhaps the most lamentable mishap that can descend on manly apparel.—They were often a little jagged at the ends. She did not understand that trousers such as these were the correct usage, they were in the tradition: he was wearing "the bearded breeches of the bard." He was a little weak on his legs, and his hands sometimes got in his own way, but she said to herself with a smile, "How different he is from other men!"

What that difference consisted in got between her and her rest, there was a crumb in her bed on the head of it.

Meanwhile, he had not told her that he loved her, and she was strangely anxious for news to that effect. Indeed, she sought confirmation of her hopes as often as maidenly modesty permitted, which was pretty frequent, for maidenly modesty has its diplomacy also; besides, has not a reigning beauty liberty to pay court?—there are plenty of other queens who have done it.

He was a poet by profession, but his livelihood depended upon his ability as a barrister. When she first saw him he was crossing a street. Suddenly, in the centre of the road, he halted, with his toes turned in, his fingers caressing his chin, and an expression of rapt and abstracted melancholy on his visage, while he sought for the missing, the transfiguring word. There was a sonnet in his eye and it impeded his vision. Meanwhile, the wheeled traffic of the street addressed language to him which was so vigorous as almost to be poetical. She had pulled him from beneath a horse's head which a frantic driver was endeavouring to pull the mouth from. The words of the driver as he sailed away were—"Go home and die, you moonstruck,

James Stephens

gibbering, wobbling omadhaun," and she had thought that his description was apt and eloquent.

She saw him a second time, when her father took her for a visit to the Four Courts. He was addressing the Court, and, while his language was magnificent, the judge must have considered that his law was on vacation, for he lost his cause.

They met again in her own home. Her father knew him very well, and, although they seldom met, he had that strong admiration for him which a vigorous and overbearing personality sometimes extends to a shy and unworldly friend—

"A perfect frost as a lawyer," he used to say, "but as a poet, sir, Shakespeare is an ass beside him, and if any one asks you who said so, tell them that I did, sir."

He sat beside her at dinner and forgot her before the first course was removed, and, later, when he knocked a glass off the table, he looked at her as though she were responsible for the debris.

He did not make love to her, a new and remarkable omission in her experience of men, however bald, and while this was refreshing for a time it became intolerable shortly. She challenged him, as a woman can, with the flash of her eyes, the quick music of her laugh, but he was marvelling at the width of the horizon, rapt in contemplation of the distant mountains, observing how a flower poised and nodded on its stalk, following the long, swooping flight of a bird or watching how the moon tramped down on the stars. So far as she could see he was unaware that her charms were of other than average significance—

"These poets are awful fools," said she angrily.

But the task of awakening this landlocked nature was one which presented many interesting features to her. She was really jealous that he paid her no attention, and, being accustomed to the homage of every male thing over fifteen years of age, she resented his negligence, became interested in him, as every one is in the abnormal, and when a woman becomes interested in a man she is unhappy until he becomes interested in her.

There had arrived, with the express intention of asking her to marry him, another young gentleman. He had a light moustache and a fancy waistcoat, both of which looked new. He was young, rich, handsome, and sufficiently silly to make any woman wish to take charge of him, and her father had told him to "go in and win, my boy, there's no one I'd like better, sir," a very good heartener for a slightly dubious youth, even though he may consider that the lady of his choice is watching another man more intently than is pleasant.

The young gentleman gripped, with careful frenzy, at his light, new moustache, and growled as he watched the stalking. But the poet was occupied and careless, and then, suddenly, it happened. What movement, conscious or unconscious, opened his eyes one cannot say: the thing seemed to be done without any preliminaries, and he was awakened and in the toils.

They had been reading poetry together, his poetry, and he was expressing, more to himself than to her, how difficult and how delightful it was to work with entire satisfaction within the scanty plot" of a sonnet. She was listening with bated breath, and answering with an animation more than slightly tinged with ignorance, for she was as little interested in the making of sonnets as in the making of shoes.—Nobody is interested in the making of sonnets, not even poets. He fell silent after a space and sat gazing at the moon where it globed out on the stillness, and she also became silent. Her nerves, she told herself, were out of order. She was more used to dismissing than to being dismissed and yet she seemed beaten. There was nothing further that a girl could do. He cared no more about her than he did about whatever woman cleaned his rooms. She was not angry, but a feeling of weariness came upon her. (It is odd that one can be so in earnest when one is in jest.) Once or twice she shook her head at the moon, and as she stared, moody and quiet, it seemed that the moon had slid beyond her vision and she was looking into great caverns of space, bursting with blackness. Some horror of emptiness was reaching to roll her in pits of murk, where her screams would be battered back on her tongue soundless.

With an effort she drew her eyes into focus again and turned them, smiling bitterly, on her companion, and, lo, he was looking at her with timid eyes, amazed eyes, and they spoke, for all their timidity, louder than trumpets. She knew that look, who could mistake it? Here was flame from the authentic fire. He was silent, but his breath came and went hurriedly, and he was bending towards her, little by little he was bending, his eyes, his whole body and soul yearning.

Then she arose—

"It is getting a little cold," said she: "we had better go in."

They went indoors silently. He was walking like a man just awakened from a dream. While she!—her head was high. Where was her equal! She frowned in the face of the moon and stars. She beat her small feet upon the earth and called it slave. She had torn victory from nowhere. A man's head swung at her girdle and she owned the blood that dripped, and her heart tossed rapture and anthem, carol and paean to the air around.—She had her hour.

That night the other young gentleman whom any woman would like to take charge of asked her to be his wife, and she consented gracefully, slightly disarranging his nice, new moustache in the act of surrender.

The next day the poet left the house pleading urgent briefs as an excuse—

"You'll come to the wedding," cried her father, "or," laughing, "maybe, you'll help us with the settlements, that's more in your line," and he put an arm fondly about his daughter. She, regarding their visitor, nestled to him and laughingly said—

"It would not be like my wedding at all if you stayed away. You must write me an ode," and her eyes mocked him.

He stood, looking at her for a moment, and his eyes mocked also, for the poet knew by his gift what she had done, and he replied with careless scorn—

"I will come with pleasure, and," with an emphasis she noted, "I will dance at your wedding." So he laughed and marched away heart-whole.

Then, disengaging her arm from her father's, she smiled and walked slowly indoors, and as she walked there spread over her body a fierce coldness, and when her husband sought her afterwards that wintry breast chilled him, and he died: but the poet danced at her wedding, when her eyes were timid and pleading, and frightened.

III

She read the letter through twice, and then she stood for a few minutes looking in front of her, with her arms hanging loosely by her sides, and her foot tapping on the carpet. She was looking into the future with the thoughtful gaze of one who has cut off all communication with the past, and, with a strange feeling of detachment, she was wondering how that future would reveal itself, and whether he. . .? She crossed to the fireplace, sat down, and read the letter over again.

Her husband had gone out that evening with a friend. In his usual hit-or-miss fashion, he kissed his wife and asked her to settle his tie. He was always asking her to do something, but he never did anything for her.—It was, "Will you hand me the paper, like a good girl?" and, "I say, dear, my pipe is stuffed, you might stick a hairpin through it," or, "You might see, old lady, if there is a match anywhere." Before their marriage she had been accustomed to men who did things for her, and the change was sudden: likeable enough at first—

. . . How red the fire is to-night! They must be sending better coal than we usually get—there is not a single dark spot in it, and how the shape continually changes! Now it is a deep cave with stalactites hanging from the roof, and little swelling hillocks on the floor, and, over all, a delicate, golden glow surging and fading. The blue flame on the top that flits and flickers like a will-o'-the-wisp is gas, I suppose—I wonder how they extract it. . . . I wonder will he be sorry when he comes home, and finds. . . . Perhaps his friend will be sufficient for him then. . . . It is curious to think of oneself as a piece of animated furniture, a dumb waiter, always ready when required, and decently out of sight when not wanted—not dumb, though! He cannot say I failed to talk about it: but, of course, that is nagging and bad temper, and "making yourself ridiculous for nothing, my dear." Nothing! I warned him over and over again; but he must have company. He would be stifled unless he went among men now and again—"Male company is a physical necessity for men, my dear." I suppose women do not need any other company than that of their husbands, and they must not ask too much of that. . . . What strange, careless, hopeful creatures they are, and how they cease to value what they have got! Does the value rise again when it is gone, I wonder? . . . Out all day, and he cannot understand why I ask him to stay with me at night. "A man wants air, sweetheart." A woman does not, of course—she would not have the cheek to want anything: there is something not "nice" about a woman wanting anything. Do all men stifle in the air their wives have breathed? If I ask him "do you love me still?" he replies, "of course, do you mind if I run out for an hour or two, dear." One will ask questions, of course. . . . A kiss in the morning, another at night, and, for Heaven's sake, don't bother me in the interval: that is marriage from a man's point of view. Do they really believe that women are alive? Is matrimony always a bondage to them? Are all women's lives so lonely? Are their wishes neglected, their attempts to think laughed at, their pride stricken?—I wonder. . . . And he did love me, I know that: but if he has forgotten I must not remember it. He could not see enough of me then: and the things he said, and does not remember—I was a wonder that the world could not equal—it is laughable.—A look from me was joy, a word delight, a touch ecstasy. He would run to the ends of the earth to gratify a whim of mine, and life without me was not worth living. . . . If I would only love him! If I could only bring myself to care for him a little—he was too humble, too unworthy to imagine—and so forth, and so forth; and it was all true then. Now I am some one who waits upon him. He wants this and that, and asks me for it. He has cut his finger and shouts for me to bind it up, and I must be terribly concerned about it; somehow, he will even manage to blame me for his cut finger. He cannot sleep in the night, so I must awaken also and listen to his complaint. He is sick, and the medicine tastes nasty; I am to understand that if the medicine tastes nasty I am responsible for it—I should not have given him anything nasty: he is surprised: he trusted me not to do such a thing to him. He turns to me like a child when he has any . . . he turns to me like a child and trusts . . . he turns to me . . . like a child. . . .

The sound of a horse's hooves came to her, and she arose from
her chair with frightened haste. She looked swiftly at the clock,
and then stood listening in a rigid attitude, with a face that
grew white and peaked, and flushed and paled again. The car
came swiftly nearer and stopped a little way from the house.
Then a foot crunched the gravel, and her desperate eyes went
roving quickly about the room as though she were looking for
a place to hide in. Next, after a little interval of silence, a
pebble struck the window. She stood for a moment staring at
the window and then ran to it, swung open a pane of glass,
and, leaning out, she called in a high, strained voice, "I will not
go." Then, closing the window again, she ran back to the
fireplace, crouched down on the rug and pushed her fingers
into her ears.

Her husband came home before eleven o'clock, brushed the
wraith of a kiss half an inch from her lips, and asked was there
anything nice for supper? The supper things were already on
the table, and, after tasting a mouthful—

"Who cooked this?" said he.

She was watching him intently—

"The girl did," she replied.

"I knew it," said he angrily, "it's beastly: you might have done
it yourself when you were not busy; a lot you care about what I
like."

"I will do it to-morrow," she replied quietly.

"Yes do," said he, "there is no one can cook like you."

And she, still watching him intently, suddenly began to
laugh—

He leaped up from the table and, after a stare of indignant astonishment, he stalked off to bed—

"You are always giggling about nothing," said he, and he banged the door.

James Stephens

THE HORSES

He was tall and she was short. He was bulky, promising to be fat. She was thin, and, with a paring here and there, would have been skinny. His face was sternly resolute, solemn indeed, hers was prim, and primness is the most everlasting, indestructible trait of humanity. It can outface the Sphinx. It is destructible only by death. Whoever has married a prim woman must hand over his breeches and his purse, he will collect postage stamps in his old age, he will twiddle his thumbs and smile when the visitor asks him a question, he will grow to dislike beer, and will admit and assert that a man's place is the home—these things come to pass as surely as the procession of the seasons.

It may be asked why he had married her, and it would be difficult to find an answer to that question. The same query might be put to almost any couple, for (and it is possibly right that it should be so) we do not marry by mathematics, but by some extraordinary attraction which is neither entirely sexual nor mental. Something other than these, something as yet uncharted by psychology, is the determining factor. It may be that the universal, strange chemistry of nature, planning granite and twig, ant and onion, is also ordering us more imperatively and more secretly than we are aware.

He had always been a hasty creature. He never had any brains, and had never felt the lack of them. He was one of those men who are called "strong," because of their imperfect control over themselves. His appetites and his mental states ruled him. He was impatient of any restraint; whatever he wanted to do he wanted urgently to do and would touch no alternatives. He had the robust good humour which will cheerfully forgive you to-morrow for the wrongs he has done you to-day. He bore no malice to any one on earth except those who took their medicine badly. Meek people got on very well with him because they behaved themselves, but he did not like them to believe they would inherit the earth.

Some people marry because other people have done so. It is in the air, like clothing and art and not eating with a knife. He, of course, got married because he wanted to, and the singular part of it was that he did not mate with a meek woman. Perhaps he thought she was meek, for before marriage there is a habit of deference on both sides which is misleading and sometimes troublesome.

From the beginning of their marriage he had fought against his wife with steadiness and even ferocity. Scarcely had they been wed when her gently-repressive hand was laid upon him, and, like a startled horse, he bounded at the touch into freedom— that is, as far as the limits of the matrimonial rope would permit. Of course he came back again—there was the rope, and the unfailing, untiring hand easing him to the way he was wanted to go.

There was no fighting against that. Or, at least, it did not seem that fighting was any use. One may punch a bag, but the bag does not mind, and at last one grows weary of unproductive quarrelling. One shrugs one's shoulders, settles to the collar, and accepts whatever destiny the gods, in their wisdom, have ordained. Is life the anvil upon which the gods beat out their will? It is not so. The anvil is matter, the will of the gods is life itself, urging through whatever torment to some identity which it can only surmise or hope for; and the one order to life is that it shall not cease to rebel until it has ceased to live; when, perhaps, it can take up the shaping struggle in some other form or some other place.

But he had almost given in. Practically he had bowed to the new order. Domestic habits were settling about him thick as cobwebs, and as clinging. His feet were wiped on the mat when he came in. His hat was hung on the orthodox projection. His kiss was given at the stated time, and lasted for the regulation period. The chimney-corner claimed him and got him. The window was his outlook on life. Beyond the hall door were foreign lands inhabited by people who were no longer of his kind. The cat and the canary, these were his familiars, and his wife was rapidly becoming his friend.

Once a day he trod solemnly forth on the designated walk—

"Be back before one o'clock," said the voice of kind authority, "lunch will be ready."

"Won't you be back before two?" said that voice, "the lawn has to be rolled."

"Don't stay out after three," the voice entreated, "we are going to visit Aunt Kate."

And at one and two and three o'clock he paced urgently wifeward. He ate the lunch that was punctually ready. He rolled the inevitable lawn. He trod sturdily to meet the Aunt Kate and did not quail, and then he went home again. One climbed to bed at ten o'clock, one was gently spoken to until eleven o'clock, and then one went to sleep.

On a day she entrusted him with a sum of money, and requested that he should go down to the town and pay at certain shops certain bills, the details whereof she furnished to him on paper.

"Be back before three o'clock," said the good lady, "for the Fegans are coming to tea. You need not take your umbrella, it won't rain, and you ought to leave your pipe behind, it doesn't look nice. Bring some cigarettes instead, and your walking-stick if you like, and be sure to be back before three."

He pressed his pipe into a thing on the wall which was meant for pipes, put his cigarette-case into his pocket, and took his walking-stick in his hand.

"You did not kiss me good-bye," said she gently.

So he returned and did that, and then he went out.

It was a delicious day. The sun was shining with all its might. One could see that it liked shining, and hoped everybody enjoyed its art. If there were birds about anywhere it is certain they were singing. In this suburb, however, there were only sparrows, but they hopped and flew, and flew and hopped, and cocked their heads sideways and chirped something cheerful, but possibly rude, as one passed. They were busy to the full extent of their beings, playing innocent games with happy little flies, and there was not one worry among a thousand of them. There was a cat lying on a hot window-ledge. She was looking drowsily at the sparrows, and any one could see that she loved them and wished them well.

There was a dog stretched across a doorway. He was very quiet, but he was not in the least bored. He was taking a sun-bath, and he was watching the cat. So steadily did he observe her that one discerned at a glance he was her friend, and would protect her at any cost.

There was a small boy who held in his left hand a tin can and a piece of string. With his right hand he was making affectionate gestures to the dog. He loved playing with animals, and he always rewarded their trust in him.

Our traveller paced slowly onwards, looking at his feet as he went. He noticed with a little dismay that he could not see as much of his legs as he thought he should see. There was a slight but nicely-shaped curve between him and his past—

"I am getting fat," said he to himself, and the reflection carried him back to the morning mirror—

James Stephens

"I am getting a bit bald, too," said he, and a quiet sadness took possession of him.

But he reassured himself. One does get fat. "Every one gets fat," said he, "after he gets married." He reviewed his friends and acquaintances, and found that this was true, and he bowed before an immutable decree.

"One does get bald," quoth he. "Everybody gets bald. The wisest people in the world lose their hair. Kings and generals, rich people and poor people, they are all bald! It is not a disgrace," said he; and he trod soberly forward in the sunshine.

A young man caught up on him from behind, and strode past. He was whistling. His coat-tails were lifted and his hands were thrust in his pockets. His elbows jerked to left and right as he marched.

"A fellow oughtn't to swagger about like that," said our traveller. "What does he want to tuck up his coat for, anyhow? It's not decent," said he in a low voice. "It makes people laugh," said he.

A girl came out of a shop near by and paced down in their direction. She looked at the young man as they passed, and then she turned again, a glance, no more, and looked after him without stopping her pace. She came on. She had no pockets to stick her hands in, but she also was waggering. There was a left and right movement of her shoulders, an impetus and retreat of her hips. Something very strong and yet reticent about her surging body. She passed the traveller and went down the road.

"She did not look at me," said he, and his mind folded its hand across its stomach, and sat down, while he went forward in the sunlight to do his errands.

He stopped to light a cigarette, and stood for a few minutes watching the blue smoke drifting and thinning away on the air. While he stood a man drove up with a horse and car. The car was laden with groceries—packets of somebody's tea, boxes of somebody's chocolate, bottles of beer and of mineral water, tins of boot blacking, and parcels of soap; confectionery, and tinned fish, cheese, macaroni, and jam.

The man was beating the horse as he approached, and the traveller looked at them both through a wreath of smoke.

"I wonder," said he, "why that man beats his horse?"

The driver was sitting at ease. He was not angry. He was not impatient. There was nothing the matter with him at all. But he was steadily beating the horse; not harshly, gently in truth. He beat the horse without ill-will, almost without knowing he was doing it. It was a sort of wrist exercise. A quick, delicate twitch of the whip that caught the animal under the belly, always in the same place. It was very skilful, but the driver was so proficient in his art that one wondered why he had to practice at it any longer. And the horse did not make any objection! Not even with his ears; they lay back to his mane as he jogged steadily forward in the sunlight. His hooves were shod with iron, but they moved with an unfaltering, humble regularity. His mouth was filled with great, yellow teeth, but he kept his mouth shut, and one could not see them. He did not increase or diminish his pace under the lash; he jogged onwards, and did not seem to mind it.

The reins were jerked suddenly, and the horse turned into the path and stopped, and when he stood he was not any quieter than when he had been moving. He did not raise his head or whisk his tail. He did not move his ears to the sounds behind and on either side of him. He did not paw and fumble with his feet. There was a swarm of flies about his head; they moved along from the point of his nose to the top of his forehead, but mostly they clustered in black, obscene patches about his eyes, and through these patches his eyes looked out with a strange patience, a strange mildness. He was stating a fact over and over to himself, and he could not think of anything else—

James Stephens

"There are no longer any meadows in the world," said he. "They came in the night and took away the green meadows, and the horses do not know what to do." . . . Horse! Horse! Little horse! . . . You do not believe me. There are those who have no whips. There are children who would love to lift you in their arms and stroke your head. . . .

The driver came again, he mounted to his seat, and the horse turned carefully and trotted away.

The man with the cigarette looked after them for a few minutes, and then he also turned carefully, to do his errands.

He reached the Railway Station and peered in at the clock. There were some men in uniform striding busily about. Three or four people were moving up the steps towards the ticket office. A raggedy man shook a newspaper in his face, paused for half a second, and fled away bawling his news. A red-faced woman pushed hastily past him. She was carrying a big basket and a big baby. She was terribly engrossed by both, and he wondered if she had to drop one which of them it would be. A short, stout, elderly man was hoisting himself and a great leather portmanteau by easy stages up the steps. He was very determined. He bristled at everybody as at an enemy. He regarded inanimate nature as if he was daring it to move. It would not be easy to make that man miss a train. A young lady trod softly up the steps. She draped snowy garments about her, but her ankles rebelled: whoever looked quickly saw them once, and then she spoke very severely to them, and they hid themselves. It was plain that she could scarcely control them, and that they would escape again when she wasn't looking. A young man bounded up the steps; he was too late to see them, and he looked as if he knew it. He stared angrily at the girl, but she lifted her chin slightly and refused to admit that he was alive. A very small boy was trying to push a large india-rubber ball into his mouth, but his mouth was not big enough to hold it, and he wept because of his limitations. He was towed along by his sister, a girl so tall that one might say her legs reached to heaven, and maybe they did.

He looked again at the hour. It was one minute to two o'clock; and hen something happened. The whole white world became red. The oldest seas in the world went suddenly lashing into storm. An ocean of blood thundered into his head, and the noise of that primitive flood, roaring from what prehistoric gulfs, deafened him at an instant. The waves whirled his feet from under him. He went foaming up the steps, was swept violently into the ticket office, and was swirled away like a bobbing cork into the train. A guard tried to stop him, for the train was already taking its pace, but one cannot keep out the tide with a ticket-puncher. The guard was overwhelmed, caught in the backwash, and swirled somewhere, anywhere, out of sight and knowledge. The train gathered speed, went flying out of the station into the blazing sunlight, picked up its heels and ran, and ran, and ran; the wind leaped by the carriage window, shrieking with laughter; the wide fields danced with each other, shouting aloud

"The horses are coming again to the green meadows. Make way, make way for the great, wild horses!"

And the trees went leaping from horizon to horizon shrieking and shrieking the news.

MISTRESS QUIET-EYES

While I sit beside the window
I can hear the pigeons coo,
That the air is warm and blue,
And how well the young bird flew—
Then I fold my arms and scold the heart
That thought the pigeons knew.

While I sit beside the window
I can watch the flowers grow
Till the seeds are ripe and blow
To the fruitful earth below—
Then I shut my eyes and tell my heart
The flowers cannot know.
While I sit beside the window
I am growing old and drear;
Does it matter what I hear,
What I see, or what I fear?
I can fold my hands and hush my heart
That is straining to a tear.

The earth is gay with leaf and flower,
The fruit is ripe upon the tree,
The pigeons coo in the swinging bower,
But I sit wearily
Watching a beggar-woman nurse
A baby on her knee.

THREE LOVERS WHO LOST

I

Young Mr. O'Grady was in love. It was the first time he had been in love, and it was all sufficiently startling. He seemed to have leaped from boyhood to manhood at a stroke, and the things which had pretended to be of moment yesterday were to-day discovered to have only the very meanest importance. Different affairs now occupied him. A little while ago his cogitations had included, where he would walk to on the next Sunday, whether his aunt in Meath Street would lend him the price of a ticket for the coming Bank Holiday excursion, whether his brother would be using his bicycle on Saturday afternoon, and whether the packet of cigarettes which he was momently smoking contained as many cigarettes as could be got elsewhere for two pence.

These things were no longer noteworthy. Clothing had assumed an importance he could scarcely have believed in. Boots, neck-ties, the conduct of one's hat and of one's head, the progress of one's moustache, one's bearing towards people in the street and in the house, this and that social observance— all these things took on a new and important dignity. He bought a walking-stick, a card-case, a purse, a pipe with a glass bottom wherein one could observe one's own nicotine inexorably accumulating.—He bought a book on etiquette and a pot of paste for making moustaches grow in spite of providence, and one day he insisted on himself drinking a half glass of whisky—it tasted sadly, but he drank it without a grimace. Etiquette and whisky! these things have to be done, and one might as well do them with an air. He was in love, he was grown up, he was a man, and he lived fearlessly up to his razor and his lady.

From the book on etiquette he exhumed a miscellany of useful and peculiar wisdom. Following information about the portage of knives and forks at incredible dinners he discovered that a well-bred person always speaks to the young lady's parents before he speaks to the young lady. He straightened his shoulders.—It would be almost as bad, he thought, as having to drink whisky, but if it had to be done why he would not shrink from this any more than he had from that. He set forth on the tingling errand.

Mr. O'Reilly was a scrivener, a husband and a father. He made copies of all kinds of documents for a living. He also copied maps. It has been said that scriveners have to get drunk at least twice a week in order to preserve their sanity; but the person whose miserable employment is to draw copies of maps is more desperately environed than an ordinary scrivener. It was Mr. O'Reilly's misfortune that he was unable to get drunk. He disliked liquor, and, moreover, it disagreed with him. He had, to paraphrase Lamb, toiled after liquor as other people toil after virtue, but the nearer he got the less did he like it. As a consequence of this enforced decency the ill-temper, which is the normal state of scriveners, had surged and buzzed around him so long that he had quite forgotten what a good temper was like.—It might be said that he hated every one, not excepting his wife and daughter. He could avoid other people, but these he could never escape from. They wanted to talk to him when he wanted to be let alone. They worried him with this and that domestic question or uproar. He would gladly have sold them both as slaves to the Barbadoes or presented them to the seraglio of any eastern potentate. There they were! and he often gnashed his teeth and grinned at them in amazement because they were there.

On the evening when young Mr. O'Grady sallied forth to ask him for the hand of his daughter in marriage he was sitting at supper with his consort—

Mr. O'Reilly took the last slice of bread from under his wife's hand. It was loot, so he ate it with an extra relish and his good lady waddled away to get more bread from cupboard—

"Everything's a trouble," said she, as she cut the loaf. "Doesn't it make you think of the hymn 'I'm but a stranger here, heaven is my home'?"

"No, ma'm," said her husband, "it does not. Where is Julia Elizabeth?" and he daringly and skilfully abstracted the next slice of bread while his wife was laying down the butter knife.

"I wish," said she, as she reached for the knife again, "I wish you would give me a chance, O'Reilly: you eat much quicker than I do, God help me!"

"I wish," rapped her husband fiercely, "that you would give a plain answer to a plain question. Now then, ma'm, in two words, where is that girl? My whole life seems to be occupied in asking that question, and yours seems to be spent in dodging the answer to it." "I don't know," replied his wife severely, "and that's three words."

"You don't know!" he looked around in helpless appeal and condemnation. "What sort of an answer is that for a mother to give about her daughter?" and under cover of his wrath he stole the next slice of bread.

His wife also became angry—she put her plate in her lap and sat up at him—

"Don't barge me, man," said she. "A nice daughter to have to give such an answer about. Leave me alone now for I'm not well, I say, on the head of her. I never know where she does be. One night it's (she endeavoured to reproduce her daughter's

James Stephens

soprano) 'I am going to a dance, mother, at the Durkins'—'"

"Ha'penny hops!" said her husband fiercely. "Can't you cut me a bit of bread!"

"And another night, 'she wants to go out to see Mary Durkan.'"

"I know her well, a big hat and no morals, a bankrupt's baggage."

"And the night after she 'wants to go to the theatre, ma.'"

"Dens of infamy," said he. "If I had my way I'd shut them all up and put the actors in gaol, with their hamleting and gamyacting and ha-ha'ing out of them."

"I can't keep her in," said his wife, wringing her hands, "and I won't try to any longer. I get a headache when I talk to her, so I do. Last night when I mentioned about her going out with that Rorke man she turned round as cool as you please and told me 'to shut up.' Her own mother!" and she surveyed Providence with a condemnatory eye—

At this point her husband swung his long arm and arrested the slice of bread in his wife's lap—

"If she spoke to me that way," he grinned, "I'll bet I'd astonish her."

His wife looked in amazement from her lap to his plate, but she had ability for only one quarrel at a time—

"And doesn't she talk to you like that? You never say a word to her but she has a look in her eye that's next door to calling you a fool.—I don't know where she is at all to-day."

"What time did she go out?"

"After breakfast this morning."

"And now it's supper-time—ha! that's good! Can't you give me a bit of bread, or do you want to eat the whole loaf yourself? Try to remember that I do pay for my food."

With an angry shake of the head his wife began to cut the loaf, and continued speaking—

"'Where are you going to, Julia Elizabeth?' said I. 'Out,' said she, and not another word could I get from her. Her own mother, mind you, and her best clothes—"

Mr. O'Reilly ate the last slice of bread and arose from the table.

"I suppose," said he, "she is loafing about the streets with some young puppy who has nothing of his own but a cigarette and a walking-stick, and they both borrowed. I'll have a talk with her when she comes in, and we'll see if she tells me to shut up."

The door banged, the room shook, and Mrs. O'Reilly settled to her frustrated tea, but her thoughts still ran on her daughter.

It was at this point that, directed by love and etiquette, Mr. O'Grady knocked at the door. Mrs. O'Reilly was again cutting the loaf in an exasperation which was partly hunger and partly maternal, and, as she cut, she communed with herself—

"As if," said she, "I haven't enough trouble trying to keep a cranky man like her pa in good humour, without being plagued by Julia Elizabeth"—she paused, for there was a knock at the door.—"If," said she to the door, "you are a woman with ferns in a pot I don't want you, and I don't want Dublin Bay herrings, or boot-laces either, so you can go away.—The crankiness of that man is more than tongue can tell. As Miss Carty says, I shouldn't stand it for an hour—Come in, can't you—and well she may say it, and she a spinster without a worry under heaven but her suspicious nature and her hair falling out. And then to be treated the way I am by that girl! It'd make a saint waxy so it would.—Good heavens! can't you come in, or are you deaf or lame or what?" and in some exasperation she arose and went to the door. She looked in perplexity for one moment from her food to her visitor, but as good manners and a lady are never separate she welcomed and drew the young man inside—

"Come in, Mr. O'Grady," said she. "How are you now at all? Why it's nearly a week since you were here. Your mother's well I hope (sit down there now and rest yourself). Some people are always well, but I'm not—it's (sit there beside the window, like a good boy) it's hard to have poor health and a crotchety husband, but we all have our trials. Is your father well too? but what's the use of asking, every one's well but me. Did your aunt get the pot of jam I sent her last Tuesday? Raspberry is supposed to be good for the throat, but her throat's all right. Maybe she threw it out: I'm not blaming her if she did. God knows she can buy jam if she wants it without being beholden to any one for presents and her husband in the Post Office.— Well, well, well, I'm real glad to see you—and now, tell me all the news?"

The young man was a little embarrassed by this flood of language and its multiplicity of direction, but the interval gave him time to collect himself and get into the atmosphere.—He replied—

"I don't think there is any news to tell, ma'm. Father and mother are quite well, thank you, and Aunt Jane got the jam all right, but she didn't eat it, because—"

"I knew she didn't," said Mrs. O'Reilly with pained humility, "we all have our troubles and jam doesn't matter. Give her my love all the same, but maybe she doesn't want it either."

"You see," said the young man, "the children got at the jam before she could, and they cleaned the pot. Aunt Jane was very angry about it."

"Was she now?" said the instantly interested lady. "It's real bad for a stout person to be angry. Apoplexy or something might ensue and death would be instantaneous and cemeteries the price they are in Glasnevin and all: but the children shouldn't have eaten all the jam at once, it's bad for the stomach that way: still, God is good and maybe they'll recover."

"They don't seem much the worse for it," said he, laughing; "they said it was fine jam."

"Well they might," replied his hostess, with suppressed indignation, "and raspberries eightpence the pound in Grafton Street, and the best preserving sugar twopence-three-farthings, and coal the way it is.—Ah, no matter, God is good, and we can't live for ever."

The four seconds of silence which followed was broken by the lover—

"Is Julia Elizabeth in, ma'm?" said he timidly.

"She's not, then," was the reply. "We all have our trials, Mr. O'Grady, and she's mine. I don't complain, but I don't deserve it, for a harder working woman never lived, but there you are."

"I'm rather glad she's out," said the youth hastily, "for I wanted to speak to yourself and your husband before I said anything to her."

Mrs. O'Reilly wheeled slowly to face him—

"Did you now?" said she, "and is it about Julia Elizabeth you came over? Well, well, well, just to think of it! But I guessed it long ago, when you bought the yellow boots. She's a real good girl, Mr. O'Grady. There's many and many's the young man, and they in good positions, mind you—but maybe you don't mean that at all. Is it a message from your Aunt Jane or your mother? Your Aunt Jane does send messages, God help her!"

"It's not, Mrs. O'Reilly: it's, if I may presume to say so, about myself."

"I knew it," was the rapid and enthusiastic reply. "She's a fine cook, Mr. O'Grady, and a head of hair that reaches down to her waist, and won prizes at school for composition. I'll call himself—he'll be delighted. He's in the next room making faces at a map. Maps are a terrible occupation, Mr. O'Grady, they spoil his eyesight and make him curse—"

She ambled to the door and called urgently—

"O'Reilly, here's young Mr. O'Grady wants to see you."

Her husband entered with a pen in his mouth and looked very severely at his visitor—

"What brought you round, young man?" said he.

The youth became very nervous. He stood up stammering—

"It's a delicate subject, sir," said he, "and I thought it would only be right to come to you first."

Here the lady broke in rapturously—

"Isn't it splendid, O'Reilly! You and me sitting here growing old and contented, and this young gentleman talking to us the way he is. Doesn't it make you think of the song 'John Anderson, my Jo, John'?"

Her husband turned a bewildered but savage eye on his spouse—

"It does not, ma'm," said he. "Well," he barked at Mr. O'Grady, "what do you want?"

"I want to speak about your daughter, sir."

"She's not a delicate subject."

"No indeed," said his wife. "Never a day's illness in her life except the measles, and they're wholesome when you're young, and an appetite worth cooking for, two eggs every morning and more if she got it."

Her husband turned on her with hands of frenzy—

"Oh—!" said he, and then to their visitor, "What have you to say about my daughter?"

"The fact is, sir," he stammered, "I'm in love with her."

"I see, you are the delicate subject, and what then?"

"And I want to marry her, sir."

"That's not delicacy, that's disease, young man. Have you spoken to Julia Elizabeth about this?"

"No, sir, I wanted first to obtain your and Mrs. O'Reilly's permission to approach her."

"And quite right, too," said the lady warmly. "Isn't it delightful," she continued, "to see a young, bashful youth telling of his love for our dear child? Doesn't it make you think of Moore's beautiful song, 'Love's Young Dream,' O'Reilly?"

"It does not," her husband snapped, "I never heard of the song I tell you, and I never want to."

He turned again to the youth—

"If you are in earnest about this, you have my permission to court Julia Elizabeth as much as she'll let you. But don't blame me if she marries you. People who take risks must expect accidents. Don't go about lamenting that I hooked you in, or led you on, or anything like that.—I tell you, here and now, that she has a rotten temper—"

His wife was aghast—

"For shame, O'Reilly," said she.

Her husband continued, looking steadily at her—

"A rotten temper," said he, "she gives back answers."

"Never," was Mrs. O'Reilly's wild exclamation.

"She scratches like a cat," said her husband.

"It's a falsehood," cried the lady, almost in tears.

"She is obstinate, sulky, stubborn and cantankerous."

"A tissue," said his wife. "An absolute tissue," she repeated with the firmness which masks hysteria.

Her husband continued inexorably—

"She's a gad-about, a pavement-hopper, and when she has the toothache she curses like a carman. Now, young man, marry her if you like."

These extraordinary accusations were powerless against love and etiquette—the young man stood up: his voice rang—

"I will, sir," said he steadily, "and I'll be proud to be her husband."

In a very frenzy of enthusiasm, Mrs. O'Reilly arose—

"Good boy," said she. "Tell your Aunt Jane I'll send her another pot of jam." She turned to her husband, "Isn't it delightful, O'Reilly, doesn't it make you think of the song, 'True, True Till Death'?"

Mr. O'Reilly replied grimly—

"It does not, ma'm.—I'm going back to my work."

"Be a gentleman, O'Reilly," said his wife pleadingly. "Won't you offer Mr. O'Grady a bottle of stout or a drop of spirits?"

The youth intervened hastily, for it is well to hide one's vices from one's family—

"Oh no, ma'm, not at all," said he, "I never drink intoxicating liquors."

"Splendid," said the beaming lady. "You're better without it. If you knew the happy homes it has ruined, and the things the clergy say about it you'd be astonished. I only take it myself for the rheumatism, but I never did like it, did I, O'Reilly?"

"Never, ma'm," was his reply. "I only take it myself because my hearing is bad. Now, listen to me, young man. You want to marry Julia Elizabeth, and I'll be glad to see her married to a sensible, sober, industrious husband.—When I spoke about her a minute ago I was only joking."

"I knew it all the time," said his wife. "Do you remember, Mr. O'Grady, I winked at you?"

"The girl is a good girl," said her husband, "and well brought up."

"Yes," said his wife, "her hair reaches down to her waist, and she won a prize for composition—Jessica's First Prayer, all about a girl with—"

Mr. O'Reilly continued—

"She brings me up a cup of tea every morning before I get up."

"She never wore spectacles in her life," said Mrs. O'Reilly, "and she got a prize for freehand drawing."

"She did so," said Mr. O'Reilly.

His wife continued—

"The Schoolboy Baronet it was; all about a young man that broke his leg down a coal mine and it never got well again until he met the girl of his heart."

"Tell me," said Mr. O'Reilly, "how are you young people going to live, and where?"

His wife interpolated—

"Your Aunt Jane told me that you had seventeen shillings and sixpence a week.—Take my advice and live on the south side—two rooms easily and most salubrious."

The young man coughed guardedly, he had received a rise of wages since that information passed, but candour belongs to childhood, and one must live these frailties down—

"Seventeen and six isn't very much, of course," said he, "but I am young and strong—"

"It's more than I had," said his host, "when I was your age. Hello, there's the post!"

Mrs. O'Reilly went to the door and returned instantly with a letter in her hand. She presented it to her husband—

"It's addressed to you, O'Reilly," said she plaintively. "Maybe it's a bill, but God's good and maybe it's a cheque."

Her husband nodded at the company and tore his letter open. He read it, and, at once as it appeared, he went mad, he raved, he stuttered, now slapping the letter with his forefinger and, anon, shaking his fist at his wife—

"Here's your daughter, ma'm," he stammered. "Here's your daughter, I say."

"Where?" cried the amazed lady. "What is it, O'Reilly?" She arose hastily and rolled towards him.

Mr. O'Reilly repelled her fiercely—

"A good riddance," he shouted.

"Tell me, O'Reilly, I command you," cried his wife.

"A minx, a jade," snarled the man.

"I insist," said she. "I must be told. I'm not well, I tell you. My head's going round. Give me the letter."

Mr. O'Reilly drew about him a sudden and terrible calmness—

"Listen, woman," said he, "and you too, young man, and be thankful for your escape."

"DEAR PA," he read, "this is to tell you that I got married to-day to Christie Rorke. We are going to open a little fried-fish shop near Amiens Street. Hoping this finds you as it leaves me at present, your loving daughter,

"JULIA ELIZABETH.

"P.S.—Give Christie's love to Ma."

Mrs. O'Reilly sank again to her chair.

Her mouth was partly open. She breathed with difficulty. Her eyes were fixed on space, and she seemed to be communing with the guardians of Chaos—

"Married!" said she in a musing whisper. "Christie!" said she.

She turned to her husband—"What an amazing thing. Doesn't it make you think, O'Reilly, of the poem, 'The World Recedes, it Disappears'?"

"It does not, ma'm," said her husband savagely.

"And what is this young gentleman going to do?" she continued, gazing tearfully at the suitor.

"He's going to go home," replied her husband fiercely. "He ought to be in bed long ago."

"A broken heart," said his wife, "is a sad companion to go home with. Doesn't it make you think of the song—?"

"It does not, ma'm," roared her husband. "I'm going back to my work," and once again the door banged and the room shook.

Young Mr. O'Grady arose timidly. The world was swimming about him. Love had deserted him, and etiquette was now his sole anchor; he shook hands with Mrs. O'Reilly—

"I think I had better be going now," said he. "Good-bye, Mrs. O'Reilly."

"Must you really go?" said that lady with the smile of a maniac.

"I'm afraid so," and he moved towards the door.

"Well," said she, "give my love to your mother and your Aunt Jane."

"I will," was his reply, "and," with firm politeness, "thank you for a very pleasant evening."

"Don't mention it, Mr. O'Grady. Good-bye."

Mrs. O'Reilly closed the door and walked back towards the

table smiling madly. She sank into a chair. Her eye fell on the butter-knife—

"I haven't had a bit to eat this day," said she in a loud and threatening voice, and once again she pulled the loaf towards her.

James Stephens

II

His mother finished reading the story of the Beautiful Princess, and it was surely the saddest story he had ever heard. He could not bear to think of that lovely and delicate lady all alone in the great, black forest waiting until the giant came back from killing her seven brothers. He would return with their seven heads swinging pitifully from his girdle, and, when he reached the castle gates, he would gnash his teeth through the keyhole with a noise like the grinding together of great rocks, and would poke his head through the fanlight of the door, and say, fee-faw-fum in a voice of such exceeding loudness that the castle would be shaken to its foundation.

Thinking of this made his throat grow painful with emotion, and then his heart swelled to the most uncomfortable dimensions, and he resolved to devote his whole life to the rescue of the Princess, and, if necessary, die in her defence.

Such was his impatience that he could not wait for anything more than his dinner, and this he ate so speedily that his father called him a Perfect-Young-Glutton, and a Disgrace-To-Any-Table. He bore these insults in a meek and heroic spirit, whereupon his mother said that he must be ill, and it was only by a violent and sustained outcry that he escaped being sent to bed.

Immediately after dinner he set out in search of the giant's castle. Now there is scarcely anything in the world more difficult to find than a giant's castle, for it is so large that one can only see it through the wrong end of a telescope; and, furthermore, he did not even know this giant's name. He might never have found the place if he had not met a certain old woman on the common.

She was a very nice old woman. She had three teeth, a red shawl, and an umbrella with groceries inside it; so he told her of the difficulty he was in.

She replied that he was in luck's way, and that she was the only person in the world who could assist him. She said her name was Really-and-Truly, and that she had a magic head, and that if he cut her head off it would answer any questions he asked it. So he stropped his penknife on his boot, and said he was ready if she was.

The old woman then informed him that in all affairs of this delicate nature it was customary to take the will for the deed, and that he might now ask her head anything he wanted to know—so he asked the head what was the way to the nearest giant, and the head replied that if he took the first turning to the left, the second to the right, and then the first to the left again, and if he then knocked at the fifth door on the right-hand side, he would see the giant.

He thanked the old woman very much for the use of her head, and she permitted him to lend her one threepenny-piece, one pocket-handkerchief, one gun-metal watch, one cap, and one boot-lace. She said that she never took two of anything, because that was not fair, and that she wanted these for a very particular, secret purpose, about which she dare not speak, and, as to which she trusted he would not press her, and then she took a most affectionate leave of him and went away.

He followed her directions with the utmost fidelity, and soon found himself opposite a house which, to the eyes of any one over seven years of age, looked very like any other house, but which, to the searching eye of six and three quarters, was patently and palpably a giant's castle.

He tried the door, but it was locked, as, indeed, he had expected it would be. Then he crept very cautiously, and peeped through the first floor window. He could see in quite plainly. There was a polar bear crouching on the floor, and the head looked at him so directly and vindictively that if he had not been a hero he would have fled. The unexpected is always terrible, and when one goes forth to kill a giant it is unkind of Providence to complicate one's adventure with a gratuitous and wholly unnecessary polar bear. He was, however, reassured by the sight of a heavy chair standing on the polar bear's stomach, and in the chair there sat the most beautiful woman in the world.

An ordinary person would not have understood so instantly that she was the most beautiful woman in the world, because she looked very stout, and much older than is customary with princesses—but that was owing to the fact that she was under an enchantment, and she would become quite young again when the giant was slain and three drops of his blood had been sprinkled on her brow.

She was leaning forward in the chair, staring into the fire, and she was so motionless that it was quite plain she must be under an enchantment. From the very first instant he saw the princess he loved her, and his heart swelled with pity to think that so beautiful a damsel should be subjected to the tyranny of a giant. These twin passions of pity and love grew to so furious a strength within him that he could no longer contain himself. He wept in a loud and very sudden voice which lifted the damsel out of her enchantment and her chair, and hurled her across the room as though she had been propelled by a powerful spring.

He was so overjoyed at seeing her move that he pressed his face against the glass and wept with great strength, and, in a few moments, the princess came timidly to the window and looked out. She looked right over his head at first, and then she looked down and saw him, and her eyebrows went far up on her forehead, and her mouth opened; and so he knew that she was delighted to see him. He nodded to give her courage, and shouted three times, "Open Sesame, Open Sesame, Open Sesame," and then she opened the window and he climbed in.

The princess tried to push him out again, but she was not able, and he bade her put all her jewels in the heel of her boot and fly with him. But she was evidently the victim of a very powerful enchantment, for she struggled violently, and said incomprehensible things to him, such as "Is it a fire, or were you chased?" and "Where is the cook?" But after a little time she listened to the voice of reason, and recognised that these were legitimate and heroic embraces from which she could not honourably disentangle herself.

When her first transports of joy were somewhat abated she assured him that excessive haste had often undone great schemes, and that one should always look before one leaped, and that one should never be rescued all at once, but gradually, in order that one might become accustomed to the severe air of freedom—and he was overjoyed to find that she was as wise as she was beautiful.

He told her that he loved her dearly, and she admitted, after some persuasion, that she was not insensible to the charms of his heart and intellect, but she confessed that her love was given to another.

At these tidings his heart withered away within him, and when the princess admitted she loved the giant his amazement became profound and complicated. There was a rushing sound in his ears. The debris of his well-known world was crashing about him, and he was staring upon a new planet, the name of which was Incredulity. He looked round with a queer feeling of insecurity. At any moment the floor might stand up n one of its corners, or the walls might begin to flap and waggle. But none of these things happened. Before him sat the princess in an attitude of deep dejection, and her lily-white hands rested helplessly on her lap. She told him in a voice that trembled that she would have married him if he had asked her ten years earlier, and urged that she could not fly with him now, because, in the first place, she had six children, and, in the second place, it would be against the law, and, in the third place, his mother might object. She admitted that she was unworthy of his love, and that she should have waited, and she bore his reproaches with a meekness which finally disarmed him.

He stropped his penknife on his boot, and said that there was nothing left but to kill the giant, and that she had better leave the room while he did so, because it would not be a sight for a weak woman, and he wondered audibly how much hasty-pudding would fall out of the giant if he stabbed him right to the heart. The princess begged him not to kill her husband, and assured him that this giant had not got any hasty-pudding in his heart at all, and that he was really the nicest giant that ever lived, and, further, that he had not killed her seven brothers, but the seven brothers of quite another person entirely, which was only a reasonable thing to do when one looked at it properly, and she continued in a strain which proved to him that this unnatural woman really loved the giant.

It was more in pity than in anger that he recognised the impossibility of rescuing this person. He saw at last that she was unworthy of being rescued, and told her so. He said bitterly that he had grave doubts of her being a princess at all, and that if she was married to a giant it was no more than she deserved, and further he had a good mind to rescue the giant from her, and he would do so in a minute, only that it was against his principles to rescue giants.—And, saying so, he placed his penknife between his teeth and climbed out through the window again.

He stood for a moment outside the window with his right hand extended to the sky and the moonlight blazing on his penknife—a truly formidable figure, and one which the princess never forgot; and then he walked slowly away, hiding behind a cold and impassive demeanour a mind that was tortured and a heart that had plumbed most of the depths of human suffering.

III

Aloysius Murphy went a-courting when the woods were green. There were grapes in the air and birds in the river. A voice and a song went everywhere, and the voice said, "Where is my beloved?" and the song replied, "Thy beloved is awaiting thee, and she stretches her hands abroad and laughs for thy coming; bind then the feather of a bird to thy heel and a red rose upon thy hair, and go quickly."

So he took his hat from behind the door and his stick from beside the bed and went out into the evening.

He had been engaged to Miss Nora MacMahon for two ecstatic months, and held the opinion that the earth and the heavens were aware of the intensity of his passion, and applauded the unique justice of his choice.

By day he sat humbly in a solicitor's office, or scurried through the thousand offices of the Four Courts, but with night came freedom, and he felt himself to be of the kindred of the gods and marched in pomp. By what subterranean workings had he become familiar with the lady? Suffice it that the impossible is possible to a lover. Everything can be achieved in time. The man who wishes to put a mountain in his pocket can do so if his pocket and his wish be of the requisite magnitude.

Now the lady towards whom the raging torrent of his affections had been directed was the daughter of his employer, and this, while it notated romance, pointed also to tragedy. Further, while this fact was well within his knowledge, it was far from the cognizance of the lady. He would have enlightened her on the point, but the longer he delayed the revelation, the more difficult did it become. Perpetually his tongue ached to utter the truth. When he might be squeezing her hand or plunging his glance into the depths of her eyes, consciousness would touch him on the shoulder with a bony hand and say, "That is the boss's daughter you are hugging"—

a reminder which was provocative sometimes of an almost unholy delight, when to sing and dance and go mad was but natural; but at other times it brought with it moods of woe, abysses of blackness.

In the solitude of the room wherein he lodged he sometimes indulged in a small drama, wherein, as the hero, he would smile a slightly sad and quizzical smile, and say gently, "Child, you are Mr. MacMahon's daughter, I am but his clerk"—here the smile became more sady quizzical—"how can I ask you to forsake the luxury of a residence in Clontarf for the uncongenial, nay, bleak surroundings of a South Circular Road habitation?" And she, ah me! She vowed that a hut and a crust and the love of her heart. . .! No matter!

So, nightly, Aloysius Murphy took the tram to Clontarf, and there, wide-coated and sombreroed like a mediaeval conspirator, he trod delicately beside his cloaked and hooded inamorata, whispering of the spice of the wind and the great stretches of the sea.

Now a lover who comes with the shades of night, harbinger of the moon, and hand in glove with the stars, must be a very romantic person indeed, and, even if he is not, a lady whose years are tender can easily supply the necessary gauze to tone down his too-rigorous projections. But the bird that flies by night must adduce for our curiosity substantial reason why his flight has deserted the whiteness of the daytime; else we may be tempted to believe that his advent in darkness is thus shrouded for even duskier purposes.—Miss MacMahon had begun to inquire who Mr. Murphy was, and he had, accordingly, begun to explain who he was not. This explanation had wrapped his identity in the most labyrinthine mystery, but Miss MacMahon detected in the rapid, incomprehensible fluctuations of his story a heart torn by unmerited misfortune, and whose agony could only be alleviated by laying her own dear head against its turmoil.

To a young girl a confidant is almost as necessary as a lover, and when the rendezvous is clandestine, the youth mysterious, and his hat broad-leafed and flapping, then the necessity for a confidant becomes imperative.

Miss MacMahon confided the knowledge of all her happiness to the thrilled ear of her younger sister, who at once hugged her, and bubbled query, conjecture, and admonishment. ". . . Long or short? . . . Dark or fair?" ". . . and slender . . . with eyes . . . dove . . . lightning . . . hair . . . and so gentle . . . and then I said . . . and then he said . . .!" "Oh, sweet!" sighed the younger sister, and she stretched her arms wide and crushed the absent excellences of Mr. Murphy to her youthful breast.

On returning next day from church, having listened awe-stricken to a sermon on filial obedience, the little sister bound her mother to secrecy, told the story, and said she wished she were dead. Subsequently the father of Clann MacMahon was informed, and he said "Hum" and "Ha," and rolled a fierce, hard eye, and many times during the progress of the narrative he interjected with furious energy these words, "Don't be a fool, Jane," and Mrs. MacMahon responded meekly, "Yes, dear," and Mr. MacMahon then said "Hum" and "Ha" and "Gr-r-r-up" in a truly terrible and ogreish manner; and in her distant chamber Miss MacMahon heard the reverberation of that sonorous grunt, and whispered to her little sister, "Pa's in a wax," and the little sister pretended to be asleep.

The spectacle of an elderly gentleman, side-whiskered, precise and grey, disguising himself with mufflers and a squash hat, and stalking with sombre fortitude the erratic wanderings of a pair of young featherheads, is one which mirth may be pleased to linger upon. Such a spectacle was now to be observed in the semi-rural outskirts of Clontarf. Mr. MacMahon tracked his daughter with considerable stealth, adopting unconsciously the elongated and nervous stride of a theatrical villain. He saw her meet a young man wearing a broad-brimmed hat, whose clothing was mysteriously theatrical, and whose general shape, when it could be glimpsed, was oddly familiar.

"I have seen that fellow somewhere," said he.

The lovers met and kissed, and the glaring father spoke rapidly but softly to himself for a few moments. He was not accustomed to walking, and it appeared as if these two intended to walk for ever, but he kept them in sight, and when the time came for parting he was close at hand.

The parting was prolonged, and renewed, and rehearsed again with amendments and additions: he could not have believed that saying good-bye to a person could be turned into so complicated and symbolic a ceremony: but, at last, his daughter, with many a backward look and wave of hand, departed in one direction, and the gentleman, after similar signals, moved towards the tramway.

"I know that fellow, whoever he is," said Mr. MacMahon.

Passing a lamp-post, Mr. Aloysius Murphy stayed for a moment to light his pipe, and Mr. MacMahon stared, he ground his teeth, he foamed at the mouth, and his already prominent eyes bulged still further and rounder—

"Well, I'm—!" said he.

He turned and walked homewards slowly, murmuring often to himself and to the night, "All right! wait, though! Hum! Ha! Gr-r-r-up!"

That night he repeatedly entreated his wife "not to be a fool, Jane," and she as repeatedly replied, "Yes, dear." Long after midnight he awoke her by roaring violently from the very interior depths of a dream, "Cheek of the fellow! Pup! Gr-r-r-up!"

At breakfast on the following morning he suggested to his wife and elder daughter that they should visit his office later on in the day—

"You have never seen it, Nora," said he, "and you ought to have a look at the den where your poor old daddy spends his time grinding dress material for his family from the faces of the poor. I've got some funny clerks, too: one of them is a curiosity." Here, growing suddenly furious, he gave an egg a clout.

His daughter giggled—

"Oh, Pa," said she, "you are not breaking that egg, you are murdering it."

He looked at her gloomily—

"It wasn't the egg I was hitting," said he. "Gr-r-r-up," said he suddenly, and he stabbed a piece of butter, squashed it to death on a slice of bread, and tore it to pieces with his teeth.

The young lady looked at him with some amazement, but she said nothing, for she believed, as most ladies do, that men are a little mad sometimes, and are foolish always.

Her father intercepted that glance, and instantly snarled—

"Can you cook, young woman?" said he.

"Of course, father," replied the perplexed maiden.

He laid aside his spoon and gave her his full attention.

"Can you cook potatoes?" said he. "Can you mash 'em, eh? Can you mash 'em? What! You can. They call them Murphies in this country, girl. Can you mash Murphys, eh? I can. There's a Murphy I know, and, although it's been mashed already, by the Lord Harry, I'll mash it again. Did you ever know that potatoes had eyes, miss? Did you ever notice it when you were cooking them? Did you ever look into the eyes of a Murphy, eh? When you mashed it, what? Don't answer me, girl."

"I don't know what you are talking about, Pa," said the young lady.

"Don't you, now?" grinned the furious gentleman, and his bulging eyes looked like little round balls of glass. "Who said you did, miss? Gr-r-r-up," said he, and the poor girl jumped as though she had been prodded with a pin.

Mr. Aloysius Murphy's activities began at ten o'clock in the morning by opening the office letters with an ivory instrument and handing them to his employer; then, as each letter was read, he entered its recept and date in a book kept for that purpose.

When Mr. MacMahon came in on the morning following the occurrences I have detailed he neglected, for the first time in many years, to respond to his clerk's respectfully-cordial salutation. To the discreet "Good-morning, sir," he vouchsafed no reply. Mr. Murphy was a trifle indignant and a good deal perturbed, for to an unquiet conscience a word or the lack of it is a goad. Once or twice, looking up from his book, he discovered his employer's hard eyes fixed upon him with a regard too particular to be pleasant.

An employer seldom does more than glance at his clerk, just the sideward glint of a look which remarks his presence without admitting his necessity, and in return the clerk slants a hurried eye on his employer, notes swiftly if his aspect be sulky or benign, and stays his vision at that. But, now, Mr. Murphy, with sudden trepidation, with a frightful sinking in the pit of his stomach, became aware that his employer was looking at him stealthily; and, little by little, he took to sneaking glances at his employer. After a few moments neither seemed to be able to keep his eyes from straying—they created opportunities in connection with the letters; the one looking intent, wide-eyed, and with a cold, frigid, rigid, hard stare, and the other scurrying and furtive, in-and-away, hit-and-miss-and-try-again, wink, blink, and twitter.

Mr. MacMahon spoke—

"Murphy!"

"Yes, sir."

"Have you anything in Court to-day?"

"Yes, sir, an ex parte application, Donald and Cluggs."

"Let O'Neill attend to it. I shall want you to draft a deed for some ladies who will call here at noon. You can come down at ten minutes after twelve."

"Yes, sir," said Murphy.

He grabbed his share of the letters and got to the door bathed in perspiration and forebodings. He closed the door softly behind him, and stood for a few seconds staring at the handle. "Blow you!" said he viciously to nothing in particular, and he went slowly upstairs.

"He can't know," said he on the first landing. On the second floor he thought, "She couldn't have told for she didn't know herself." He reached his desk. "I wish I had a half of whisky," said the young man to himself.

Before, however, twelve o'clock arrived he had journeyed on the hopeful pinions of youth from the dogmatic "could not be" to the equally immovable "is not," and his mind resumed its interrupted equilibrium.

At twelve o'clock Mrs. and Miss MacMahon arrived, and were at once shown into the private office. At ten minutes past, Mr. Murphy's respectful tap was heard. "Don't, Eddie," said Mrs. MacMahon in a queer, flurried voice. "Come in," said her husband. Nora was examining some judicial cartoons pinned over the mantelpiece. Mr. Murphy opened the door a few inches, slid through the aperture, and was at once caught and held by his employer's eye, which, like a hand, guided him to the table with his notebook. Under the almost physical pressure of that authoritative glare he did not dare to look who was in the room, but the rim of his eye saw the movement of a skirt like the far-away, shadowy canter of a ghost's robe. He fixed his attention on his note-book.

Mr. MacMahon began to dictate a Deed of Conveyance from a precedent deed in his hand. After dictating for some few minutes—

"Murphy," said he, and at the word the young lady studying the cartoons stiffened, "I've rather lost the thread of that clause; please read what you have down."

Murphy began to read, and, at the first word, the girl made a tiny, shrill, mouse's noise, and then stood stock-still, tightened up and frightened, with her two wild eyes trying to peep around her ears

Mr. Murphy heard the noise and faltered—he knew instinctively. Something told him with the bellowing assurance of a cannon who was there. He must look. He forced his slack face past the granite image that was his employer, saw a serge-clad figure that he knew, on ear and the curve of a cheek. Then a cascade broke inside his head. It buzzed and chattered and crashed, with now and again the blank brutality of thunder bashing through the noise. The serge-clad figure swelled suddenly to a tremendous magnitude, and then it receded just as swiftly, and the vast earth spun minutely on a pin's point ten million miles away, and she was behind it, her eyes piercing with scorn. . . . Through the furious winds that whirled about his brain he heard a whisper, thin and cold, and insistent as a razor's edge, "Go on, Murphy; go on, Murphy." He strove to fix his attention on his shorthand notes—To fight it down, to stand the shock like a man, and then crawl into a hole somewhere and die; but his mind would not grip, nor his eyes focus. The only words which his empty brain could pump up were these, irrelevant and idiotic, "'A frog he would a-wooing go, heigho,' said Rowley"; and they must not be said. "It is a bit difficult, perhaps," said the whispering voice that crept through the tumult of winds and waters in his head. "Never mind, take down the rest of it," and the far-away whisper began to say things all about nothing, making queer little noises and pauses, running for a moment into a ripple of sound, and eddying and dying away and coming back again— buz-z-z! His notebook lying on the table was as small as a postage stamp, while the pencil in his hand was as big as an elephant's leg. How can a man write on a microscopic blur with the stump of a fir tree? He poked and prodded, and Mr. MacMahon watched for a few moments his clerk poking his note-book with the wrong end of a pencil. He silently pulled his daughter forward and made her look. After a little—

"That will do, Murphy," said he, and Mr. Murphy, before he got out, made two severe attempts to walk through a wall.

For half an hour he sat at his desk in a trance, with his eyes fixed upon an ink-bottle. At last, nodding his head slowly—

"I'll bet you a shilling," said he to the ink-bottle, "that I get the sack to-night."

And the ink-bottle lost the wager.

THE BLIND MAN

He was one who would have passed by the Sphinx without seeing it. He did not believe in the necessity for sphinxes, or in their reality, for that matter—they did not exist for him. Indeed, he was one to whom the Sphinx would not have been visible. He might have eyed it and noted a certain bulk of grotesque stone, but nothing more significant.

He was sex-blind, and, so, peculiarly limited by the fact that he could not appreciate women. If he had been pressed for a theory or metaphysic of womanhood he would have been unable to formulate any. Their presence he admitted, perforce: their utility was quite apparent to him on the surface, but, subterraneously, he doubted both their existence and their utility. He might have said perplexedly—Why cannot they do whatever they have to do without being always in the way? He might have said—Hang it, they are everywhere and what good are they doing? They bothered him, they destroyed his ease when he was near them, and they spoke a language which he did not understand and did not want to understand. But as his limitations did not press on him neither did they trouble him. He was not sexually deficient, and he did not dislike women; he simply ignored them, and was only really at home with men. All the crudities which we enumerate as masculine delighted him—simple things, for, in the gender of abstract ideas, vice is feminine, brutality is masculine, the female being older, vastly older than the male, much more competent in every way, stronger, even in her physique, than he, and, having little baggage of mental or ethical preoccupations to delay her progress, she is still the guardian of evolution, requiring little more from man than to be stroked and petted for a while.

He could be brutal at times. He liked to get drunk at seasonable periods. He would cheerfully break a head or a window, and would bandage the one damage or pay for the other with equal skill and pleasure. He liked to tramp rugged miles swinging his arms and whistling as he went, and he could sit for hours by the side of a ditch thinking thoughts without words—an easy and a pleasant way of thinking, and one which may lead to something in the long run.

Even his mother was an abstraction to him. He was kind to her so far as doing things went, but he looked over her, or round her, and marched away and forgot her.

Sex-blindness carries with it many other darknesses. We do not know what masculine thing is projected by the feminine consciousness, and civilisation, even life itself, must stand at a halt until that has been discovered or created, but art is the female projected by the male: science is the male projected by the male—as yet a poor thing, and to remain so until it has become art; that is, has become fertilised and so more psychological than mechanical. The small part of science which came to his notice (inventions, machinery, etc.) was easily and delightedly comprehended by him. He could do intricate things with a knife and a piece of string, or a hammer and a saw: but a picture, a poem, a statue, a piece of music— these left him as uninterested as they found him: more so, in truth, for they left him bored and dejected.

His mother came to dislike him, and there were many causes and many justifications for her dislike. She was an orderly, busy, competent woman, the counterpart of endless millions of her sex, who liked to understand what she saw or felt, and who had no happiness in reading riddles. To her he was at times an enigma, and at times again a simpleton. In both aspects he displeased and embarrassed her. One has one's sense of property, and in him she could not put her finger on anything that was hers. We demand continuity, logic in other words, but between her son and herself there was a gulf fixed, spanned by no bridge whatever; there was complete isolation; no boat plied between them at all. All the kindly human things which she loved were unintelligible to him, and his coarse pleasures or blunt evasions distressed and bewildered her. When she spoke to him he gaped or yawned; and yet she did not speak on weighty matters, just the necessary small-change of existence—somebody's cold, somebody's dress, somebody's marriage or death. When she addressed him on sterner subjects, the ground, the weather, the crops, he looked at her as if she were a baby, he listened with stubborn resentment, and strode away a confessed boor. There was no contact anywhere between them, and he was a slow exasperation to her.—What can we do with that which is ours and not ours? either we own a thing or we do not, and, whichever way it goes, there is some end to it; but certain enigmas are illegitimate and are so hounded from decent cogitation.

She could do nothing but dismiss him, and she could not even do that, for there he was at the required periods, always primed with the wrong reply to any question, the wrong aspiration, the wrong conjecture; a perpetual trampler on mental corns, a person for whom one could do nothing but apologise.

They lived on a small farm and almost the entire work of the place was done by him. His younger brother assisted, but that assistance could have easily been done without. If the cattle were sick he cured them almost by instinct. If the horse was lame or wanted a new shoe he knew precisely what to do in both events. When the time came for ploughing he gripped the handles and drove a furrow which was as straight and as economical as any furrow in the world. He could dig all day long and be happy; he gathered in the harvest as another would gather in a bride; and, in the intervals between these occupations, he fled to the nearest publichouse and wallowed among his kind.

He did not fly away to drink; he fled to be among

men.—Then he awakened. His tongue worked with the best of them, and adequately too. He could speak weightily on many things—boxing, wrestling, hunting, fishing, the seasons, the weather, and the chances of this and the other man's crops. He had deep knowledge about brands of tobacco and the peculiar virtues of many different liquors. He knew birds and beetles and worms; how a weazel would behave in extraordinary circumstances; how to train every breed of horse and dog. He recited goats from the cradle to the grave, could tell the name of any tree from its leaf; knew how a bull could be coerced, a cow cut up, and what plasters were good for a broken head. Sometimes, and often enough, the talk would chance on women, and then he laughed as heartily as any one else, but he was always relieved when the conversation trailed to more interesting things.

His mother died and left the farm to the younger instead of the elder son; an unusual thing to do, but she did detest him. She knew her younger son very well. He was foreign to her in nothing. His temper ran parallel with her own, his tastes were hers, his ideas had been largely derived from her, she could track them at any time and make or demolish him. He would go to a dance or a picnic and be as exhilarated as she was, and would discuss the matter afterwards. He could speak with some cogency on the shape of this and that female person, the hat of such an one, the disagreeableness of tea at this house and the goodness of it at the other. He could even listen to one speaking without going to sleep at the fourth word. In all he was a decent, quiet lad who would become a father the exact replica of his own, and whose daughters would resemble his mother as closely as two peas resemble their green ancestors.— So she left him the farm.

Of course, there was no attempt to turn the elder brother out. Indeed, for some years the two men worked quietly together and prospered and were contented; then, as was inevitable, the younger brother got married, and the elder had to look out for a new place to live in, and to work in—things had become difficult.

It is very easy to say that in such and such circumstances a man should do this and that well-pondered thing, but the courts of logic have as yet the most circumscribed jurisdiction. Just as statistics can prove anything and be quite wrong, so reason can sit in its padded chair issuing pronouncements which are seldom within measurable distance of any reality. Everything is true only in relation to its centre of thought. Some people think with their heads—their subsequent actions are as logical and unpleasant as are those of the other sort who think only with their blood, and this latter has its irrefutable logic also. He thought in this subterranean fashion, and if he had thought in the other the issue would not have been any different.

Still, it was not an easy problem for him, or for any person lacking initiative—a sexual characteristic. He might have emigrated, but his roots were deeply struck in his own place, so the idea never occurred to him; furthermore, our thoughts are often no deeper than our pockets, and one wants money to move anywhere. For any other life than that of farming he had no training and small desire. He had no money and he was a farmer's son. Without money he could not get a farm; being a farmer's son he could not sink to the degradation of a day labourer; logically he could sink, actually he could not without endangering his own centres and verities—so he also got married.

He married a farm of about ten acres, and the sun began to shine on him once more; but only for a few days. Suddenly the sun went away from the heavens; the moon disappeared from the silent night; the silent night itself fled afar, leaving in its stead a noisy, dirty blackness through which one slept or yawned as one could. There was the farm, of course, one could go there and work; but the freshness went out of the very ground; the crops lost their sweetness and candour; the horses and cows disowned him; the goats ceased to be his friends—It was all up with him. He did not whistle any longer. He did not swing his shoulders as he walked, and, although he continued to smoke, he did not look for a particular green bank whereon he could sit quietly flooded with those slow thoughts that had no words.

For he discovered that he had not married a farm at all. He had married a woman—a thin-jawed, elderly slattern, whose sole beauty was her farm. How her jaws worked! The processions and congregations of words that fell and dribbled and slid out of them! Those jaws were never quiet, and in spite of all he did not say anything. There was not anything to say, but much to do from which he shivered away in terror. He looked at her sometimes through the muscles of his arms, through his big, strong hands, through fogs and fumes and singular, quiet tumults that raged within him. She lessoned him on the things he knew so well, and she was always wrong. She lectured him on those things which she did know, but the unending disquisition, the perpetual repetition, the foolish, empty emphasis, the dragging weightiness of her tongue made him repudiate her knowledge and hate it as much as he did her.

Sometimes, looking at her, he would rub his eyes and yawn with fatigue and wonder—there she was! A something enwrapped about with petticoats. Veritably alive. Active as an insect! Palpable to the touch! And what was she doing to him? Why did she do it? Why didn't she go away? Why didn't she die? What sense was there in the making of such a creature that clothed itself like a bolster, without any freedom or entertainment or shapeliness?

Her eyes were fixed on him and they always seemed to be angry; and her tongue was uttering rubbish about horses, rubbish about cows, rubbish about hay and oats. Nor was this the sum of his weariness. It was not alone that he was married; he was multitudinously, egregiously married. He had married a whole family, and what a family—

Her mother lived with her, her eldest sister lived with her, her youngest sister lived with her—and these were all swathed about with petticoats and shawls. They had no movement. Their feet were like those of no creature he had ever observed. One could hear the flip-flap of their slippers all over the place, and at all hours. They were down-at-heel, draggle-tailed, and futile. There was no workmanship about them. They were as unfinished, as unsightly as a puddle on a road. They insulted his eyesight, his hearing, and his energy. They had lank hair that slapped about them like wet seaweed, and they were all talking, talking, talking.

The mother was of an incredible age. She was senile with age. Her cracked cackle never ceased for an instant. She talked to the dog and the cat; she talked to the walls of the room; she spoke out through the window to the weather; she shut her eyes in a corner and harangued the circumambient darkness. The eldest sister was as silent as a deep ditch and as ugly. She slid here and there with her head on one side like an inquisitive hen watching one curiously, and was always doing nothing with an air of futile employment. The youngest was a semi-lunatic who prattled and prattled without ceasing, and was always catching one's sleeve, and laughing at one's face.—And everywhere those flopping, wriggling petticoats were appearing and disappearing. One saw slack hair whisking by the corner of one's eye. Mysteriously, urgently, they were coming and going and coming again, and never, never being silent.

More and more he went running to the public-house. But it was no longer to be among men, it was to get drunk. One might imagine him sitting there thinking those slow thoughts without words. One might predict that the day would come when he would realise very suddenly, very clearly all that he had been thinking about, and, when this urgent, terrible thought had been translated into its own terms of action, he would be quietly hanged by the neck until he was as dead as he had been before he was alive.

SWEET-APPLE

At the end of the bough, at the top of the tree
(As fragrant, as high, and as lovely as thou)
One sweet apple reddens which all men may see,
At the end of the bough.
Swinging full to the view, tho' the gatherers now
Pass, and evade, and o'erlook busily:
Overlook! nay, but pluck it! they cannot tell how.

For it swings out of reach as a cloud, and as free
As a star, or thy beauty, which seems too, I vow,
Remote as the sweet rosy apple—ah me!
At the end of the bough.

James Stephens

THREE HAPPY PLACES

I

One awakened suddenly in those days. Sleep was not followed by the haze which trails behind more mature slumbers. One's eyes opened wide and bright, and brains and legs became instantly active. If by a chance the boy lying next to you was still asleep, it was the thing to hit him with a pillow. Even among boys, however, there are certain morose creatures who are ill-tempered in the morning, and these, on being struck with a pillow, become malignantly active, and desire to fight with fists instead of pillows.

Bull was such a boy. He was densely packed with pugnacity. He lived for ever on the extreme slope of a fight, down which he slid at a word, a nod, a wink, into strenuous and bloodthirsty warfare. He was never seen without a black eye, a bruised lip, or something wrong with his ear. He had the most miscellaneous collection of hurts that one could imagine, and he was always prepared to exhibit his latest injury in exchange for a piece of toffee. If this method of barter was not relished, he would hit the proprietor of the toffee and confiscate the goods to his own use.

His knowledge of who had sweets was uncanny. He had an extra sense in that direction, which was a trouble to all smaller boys. No matter how cunningly one concealed a sticky treasure, just when one was secretly enjoying it he came leaping out of space with the most offensive friendliness crinkling all over his face, and his desire to participate in the confection was advanced without any preliminary courtesies—

"What have you got? Show! Give us a bit. Can't you give a fellow a bit?"

When the bit was tendered he snatched it, swallowed it, and growled—

"Do you call that a bit? Give us a real bit."

There are plenty of boys who will defend their toffee with their lives. Such boys he liked to meet, for their refusal to surrender a part gave him an opportunity to fight and a reason for confiscating the whole of the ravished sweetmeat. One often had to devour one's sweets at a full gallop. It was no uncommon thing to see a small boy scudding furiously around a field with Bull pounding behind, intent as a bloodhound, and as horribly vocal. A close examination would discover that the small boy's jaws were moving with even greater rapidity than his legs. If he managed to get his stuff devoured before he was caught it was all right, but he got hammered anyhow when he was caught. However, Bull's approach was usually managed with great skill and strategy, and before the small boy was aware Bull was squatting beside him using blandishments both moral and minatory.

He was a very gifted boy. He had no bent for learning lessons but he had a great gift for collecting and turning to his own use the property of other people. Sometimes three or four boys swore a Solemn League and Covenant against him. His perplexity then was extreme. He saw toffee being devoured and none of it coming his way. Possibly his method of thinking was in pictures, and he could visualise with painful clarity the alien gullets down which toffee was traveling, and, simultaneously, he could see the woeful emptiness of his own red lane. He must have felt that all was not right with a Providence which could allow such happenings. A world wherein there was toffee for others and none for him was certainly a world out of joint. His idea of Utopia would be a place where there were lots of things for him to eat and a circle of hungry boys who watched his deliberate jaws with envy and humility. Furthermore, the idea that smaller boys could have, not the courage, but the heart to congregate against him, must have come to him with a shock. He was appalled by a sense of the sinfulness of human nature, and dismayed by the odds against which virtue has to fight.

The others, strong in numbers, followed him on such occasions chewing their tuck with grave deliberation, descanting minutely and loudly on the taste of each bit, the splendid length of time it took to dissolve, and the blessedly large quantity which yet remained to be eaten. He threatened them, but his threats were received with yawns. He wheedled (a thing he could do consummately well) but they were not to be blandished. He mapped out on his own person the particular and painful places where later on he would hit them unless he was bound over to the peace by toffee. And they sucked their sweetstuff and made diagrams on each other of the places where they could hit Bull if they had a mind to, and told each other and him that he was not worth hitting and, would probably die if he were hit. But they were careful not dissolve artnership until the sweets were eaten and beyond even the wildest hopes of salvage. Then, in the later-on that had been predicted, Bull captured them in detail, and, as he had promised, he "lammed the stuffing" out of them.

He had all the grave wisdom of the stupid, and the extraordinary energy and persistence which perpetuates them. He never could learn a lesson, but he could, and did, pinch the boy next to him into adept prompting, and would intimidate any one into doing his sums. Indeed, the man of whom he was the promise had no need for ordinary learning. The lighter accomplishments of life had no appeal, nor would the deeper lessons have any meaning for him. He is simply a big, physical appetite, untrammelled by anything like introspection or conscience, and working in perfect innocence for the fulfilment of its simple wants. For at base his species are surely the most simple of human creatures. In spite of their complex physical structure they are one-celled organisms driven through life with only a passionate hunger as their motive power, and with no complexities of thought or emotion to hamper their loud progressions. None but those of their own kind can suffer from their ravages, and, even so, they fly the contact of each other with horror.

Doubtless by this time Bull is a prosperous and wealthy citizen somewhere, the proprietor of a curved waistcoat and a gold watch. Possessions other than these he would regard with the amiable tolerance of a philosopher regarding a child with toys. So strongly acquisitive a nature must win the particular little battles which it is fitted to wage. When a conscienceless mind is buttressed by a pugnacious temperament then houses and land, and cattle and maidservants, and such-like, the small change of existence, are easily gotten.

II

The sunlight of youth has a special quality which will never again be known until we rediscover it in Paradise. What a time it was! How the sun shone, and how often it shone! I remember playing about in a parched and ragged field with a leaf from a copy-book stuck under my cap to aid its quarter-inch peak in keeping off the glare of that tremendous sunshine.

Tip-and-Tig, Horneys and Robbers, Relievo we played, and another game, the name of which did not then seem at all strange, but which now wears an amazing appearance—it was, Twenty-four Yards on the Billy-Goat's Tail. I wonder now what was that Billy-Goat, and was he able to wag the triumphant tail of which twenty-four yards was probably no more than an inconsiderable moiety. There were other games: Ball-in-the-Decker, Cap-on-the-Back, and Towns or Rounders. These were all summer games.

With the lightest effort of imagination I can see myself and other tireless atoms scooting across reaches of sunlight. I can hear the continuous howl which accompanied our play, and can see that ragged, parched field spreading, save for the cluster of boys, wide and silent to the further, greener fields, where the cows were lying down in great coloured lumps, and one antic deer, a pet, would make such astonishing journeys, jumping the entire circuit of the field on four thin and absolutely rigid legs; for when it made these peculiar excursions it never seemed to use its legs—these were held quite rigidly, and the deer bounded by some powerful, spring-like action, its brown coat flashing in the sunlight, and its movement a rhythmic glory which the boys watched with ecstasy and laughter.

An old ass was native to that field also. He had been a bright, kind-hearted donkey at one time: a donkey whose nose might be tickled, and who would allow one to climb upon his back. But the presence of boys grew disturbing as he grew old, and the practical jokes of which his youth took no heed induced a kind of insanity in his latter age. He took to kicking the cows as they browsed peacefully, and, later, he developed a horrid appetite for fowl, and would stalk and kill and eat hens whenever possible. Later still he directed this unhealthy appetite towards small boys, and after he had eaten part of one lad's shoulder and the calf from another boy's leg he disappeared—whether he was sold to some innocent person, or had been slaughtered mysteriously, we did not know. We professed to believe that he had died of the horrible taste of the boys he had bitten, and, afterwards, whenever we played cannibals, we refused, greatly to their chagrin, to kill and eat these two boys, on the ground that their flesh was poisonous; but the others we slaughtered and fed on with undiminished gusto.

There were only two trees in the field—great, gnarled monsters casting a deep shade. In that shade the grass grew long and green and juicy. After a game the boys would fling themselves down in the shadow of the trees to chew the sweet grass, and play "knifey," and talk.—Such talk!—endless and careless, and loud as the converse of young bulls. What did we talk about? Delightful and inconsequent shoutings—

"That is a hawk up there, he's going to soar. How does he keep so steady without moving his wings? Watch now! down he drops like a stone. . . . If you give your rabbit too many cabbage leaves he'll die of the gripes. . . . Did you ever play jack-stones? a fellow showed me how, look! . . . When we were at the sea yesterday Jimmy Nelson wouldn't go out from the shore. He was afraid of his life—he wouldn't even duck down. I swam nearly out of sight, didn't I, Sam? So did Sam. . . . You could climb right up to the top of that tree if you tried. No you couldn't.—Yes I could, it's forked all the way up. . . . The new master wears specs—Old Four-Eyes! and he grins at a fellow. I don't think he's much. . . . How do midges get born? . . . My brother has one with four blades and a thing for poking stones out of a horse's hoof. . . . A horse-hair won't break the cane at all: it's all bosh: rosin is the only thing. . . ."

James Stephens

There was a little stream which twisted a six-foot path through the field, the sunshine dashing off its waters in brilliant flashes. The top of the water swarmed with flying insects and strange, small spider-things skimmed over its surface with amazing swiftness. We believed there were otters in that stream—they came out at nightfall and, unless you had the good fortune to be rescued by a Newfoundland dog, they would hold you down under water until you were drowned. We also held there were leeches in the stream—they would grip you by the hundred thousand and suck you to death in five minutes, and they clung so tightly that one could not prise their mouths open with a poker. We hoped there were whales in it, but not one of us desired a shark because it is the Sailor's Enemy.

An iron railing ran by part of the field. Every hole and joint of it was crammed with earwigs, and these could be poked out of the crevices with a straw. When an amazing number of them had been poked out there was always another one left. The very last earwig that could be discovered was the King. He was able and willing to bite ten times as badly as any of the others, and he was awfully vicious when his nest was broken into. Furthermore, he had the ability to put a curse on you before he died, and he always did this because he was so vicious. If a King Earwig had time to curse you before he was killed terrible things might happen. His favourite curse was to translate himself into the next piece of bread you would eat, and then you would see one-half of him waggling in a hole in the bread: the other half you had already eaten.—For this reason the King Earwig was always allowed to go free until he was not looking, then he was killed with great suddenness.

I remember how the slow evening shadows drew over the quiet fields. The sunlight slowly faded to a mist of gold, into which the great trees thrust timorous, shy fingers, and these gradually widened, until, at last, the whole horizon bowed into the twilight.

Across the field there could be heard the voice of the river, afurtive, desolate hoarseness in the dusk. The cows in the far fields had long ago wandered home to be milked, scarcely a bird moved in the high silences, the gnats had hidden themselves away in the deep, rugged bark of the trees, and, through the dimness, the heavy beetles were hurling like stones, and dropping and rising again in a laborious flight.

III

He could remember that he had wept to be allowed go to school. Even more vivid was his recollection of the persuasive and persistent tears which he had shed to be allowed to stay at home.

Most of the joys of school were exhausted after he had submitted to one hour of dreary discipline.—To be compelled to sit still when every inch of one's being clamoured to move about; to have to stand up and stare at a blackboard upon which meaningless white scrawls were perpetually being drawn, and as perpetually being wiped out to a master's meaningless, monotonous verbal accompaniment; to have to join in a chant which began with "a, b, c," and droned steadily through a complexity of sounds to a ridiculously inadequate "z"—such things became desperately boring. One was not even let go to sleep, and if one wept from sheer ennui, then one was clouted. School, he shortly decided, was not worth anybody's while, but he also discovered that a torment had commenced which was not by any artifice to be evaded.

Along the road to school there ran a succession of meadows—the path was really a footway through fields—and how not to stray into these meadows was a problem demanding the entire of one's attention. Sometimes a rabbit bolted almost from under one's feet—it flapped away through the grass, and bobbed up and down in a great hurry. Then his heart filled with envy. He said to himself—

"That rabbit is not going to school: if it was it wouldn't run so quickly."

It was paltry comfort to hurl a wad of grass after it.

Through most of the journey there was an immense, lazy bee with a bass voice, and he droned defiance three feet away from one's cap which almost jolted to be put over him. He seemed to understand that at such an hour he was not in any danger, and so he would drop to the grass, roll on his back, and cock up his legs in ecstasy.

"Bees," said he to himself in amazement and despair, "do not go to school."

Each bus h and tree seemed, for the moment, to be inhabited by a bird whose song was unfamiliar and the markings on whom he could not remember to have seen before; and he had no time to stay and note them. He dragged beyond these objects reluctantly, pondering on the unreasonable savagery of parents who sent one to school when the sun was shining.

But the greatest obstacle to getting to school was the river which danced briskly through the fields. The footpath went for a stretch along this stream, and, during that piece of the journey, haste was not possible. There are so many things in a river to look at. The movement of the water in itself exercises fascinations over a boy. There are always bubbles, based strongly in froth, sailing gallantly along.—One speculates how long a bubble will swim before it hits a rock, or is washed into nothing by an eddy, or is becalmed in a sheltered corner to ride at jaunty anchor with a navy of similar delicate tonnage.

Further, if one finds a twig on the path, or a leaf, there is nothing more natural than to throw these into the river and see how fast or how erratically they sail. Pebbles also clamour to be cast into the stream. Perhaps a dragon-fly whirls above the surface of the water to hold one late from school. The grasses and rushes by the marge may stir as a grey rat slips out to take to the water and swim low down and very fast on some strange and important journey. The inspection of such an event cannot be hurried. One must, if it is possible, discover where he swims to, and if his hole is found it has to be blocked up with stones, even though the persistent bell is clanging down over the fields.

Perhaps a big frog will push out from the grass and go in fat

James Stephens

leaps down to the water—plop! and away he swims with his sarcastic nose up and his legs going like fury. The strange, very-little-boy motions of a frog in water is a thing to ponder over. There are small frogs also, every bit as interesting, thin-legged, round-bellied anatomies who try to jump two ways at once when they are observed, and are caught so easily that it is scarcely worth one's trouble to chase them at all.

Just where the path turned there was an arch under which the river flowed.—It was covered in with an iron grating. Surely it was a place of mystery. Through the bars the dark, swirling waters were dimly visible—there were things in there. Black lumps rose out of the water, and, for a little distance, the slimy, shimmering, cold-looking walls could be seen. Beyond there was a deeper gloom, and, beyond that again, a blank, mysterious darkness. Through the grating the voice of the stream came back with a strange note. On the outside, under the sun, it was a tinkle and a rush, a dance indeed, but within it was a low snarl that deepened to a grim whisper. There was an edge of malice to the sound: something dark and very terrible brooded on the face of those hidden waters. It was the home of surmise.—What might there not be there? There might be gully-holes where the waters whirled in wide circles, and then flew smoothly down, and down, and down. If one could have got in there to see! To crawl along by the slippery edge in the darkness and solitude! It was very hard to get away from this place.

A little farther on two goats were tethered. As one passed they would cease to pluck the grass and begin to dance slowly, such dainty, antic steps, with their heads held down and their pale eyes looking upwards with a joke in them. They did not really want to fight; they wanted to play but were too shy to admit it.

And here the schoolhouse was in sight. The bell had stopped: it was now time to run.

He gripped the mouth of his satchel with one hand to prevent the lesson books from jumping out as he ran, he gripped his pocket with the other hand to prevent his lunch from being jolted into the road.

Another few yards and he was at the gate—some one was glaring out through a window. It was a big face rimmed with spectacles and whiskers—a master. He knew that when yonder severe eye had lifted from him it had dropped to look at a watch, and he also knew exactly what the owner of the severe eye would say to him as he sidled in.

THE MOON

If the Moon had a hand
I wonder would she
Stretch it down unto me?

If she did, I would go
To her glacier land,
To her ice-covered strand.

I would run, I would fly,
Were the cold ever so,
And be warm in the snow.

O Moon of all Light,
Sailing far, sailing high
In the infinite sky.

Do not come down to me,
Lest I shriek in affright,
Lest I die in the night
Of your chill ecstasy.

THERE IS A TAVERN IN THE TOWN

I

The old gentleman entered, and was about to sit down, when a button became detached from some portion of his raiment and rolled upon the floor. He picked the button up and observed that he would keep it for his housekeeper to sew on, and, while speaking on the strangeness of housekeeping and buttons, he came slowly to the subject of matrimony—

"Like so many other customs," said he, "marriage is not native to the human race, nor is it altogether peculiar to it. So far as I am aware no person was ever born married, and in extreme youth bachelors and spinsters are so common as to call for no remark. Nature strives, not for duality as in the case of the Siamese Twins but for individuality. We are all born strongly separated, and I am often inclined to fancy that this ceremony of joining appears very like flying in the face of Providence. I have also thought, on the other hand, that the segregation of humanity into male and female is not an economic practice, but I fear the foundation of the sex habit is by this time so deeply trenched in our natures as to be practically ineradicable.

"Throughout nature the male and female habit is usual: all beasts are born of one or the other gender, and this is also the case in the vegetable kingdom: but I am not aware that the ridiculous and wasteful preparations with which we encumber matrimony obtain also among plants and animals. Certainly,

James Stephens

among some animals courtship, as we understand it, is practi-ed—Wolves, for instance, are an extraordinarily acute people who make good husbands and fathers, and in these relations they display a tenderness and courtesy which one only acquainted with their out-of-door manners would scarcely credit them with. Their courtship is conducted under circumstances of extraordinary rigour. A he-wolf who becomes enamoured of a female from another tribe is forced, in attempting to wed her, to set his life upon the venture, and, disdaining all the fury of her numerous relatives, he must forcibly detach her from her family, kill or maim all her other suitors, sustain n a wounded and desperate condition a prolonged chase over the now-clad Russian Steppes, and, ultimately, consummate his nuptials, if he can, with as many limbs as his lady's family have failed to collect off him. This is a courtship admirably fitted to evolve a hardy and Spartan race strong in the virtues of reliance and self-control.

"Spiders, on the other hand, are a people whom I despise on several counts, but must admire on others. They conduct their love affairs in an even more tragic style. In every event matrimony is a tragedy, but in the case of spiders it is a catastrophe. Spiders are a very sour and pessimistic people who live in walls, corners of hotel bedrooms and holes generally, in which places they weave very delicate webs, and sit for a long period in a state of philosophic ecstasy, contemplating the infinite. Their principal pastimes are killing flies and committing suicide—both of which games should be encouraged. Like so many other unhappy creatures they are born with a gender from which there is no escape. The male spider is very much smaller than the female, and he does not care greatly for his life. When he does not desire to live any longer he commits matrimony or suicide. He weds a large and fierce wife, who, when in expectation of progeny, kills him, and, being a thorough-going person as all females are, she also eats him, possibly at his own request, and thus she relieves her husband of the tedium of existence and herself of the necessity for seeking immediate victual. I do not know whether male spiders are very plentiful or extremely scarce, but I cite this as an example of the extravagance and economy of the female gender.

"Of the courting habits of fish I have scanty knowledge. Fish are very ugly, dirty creatures who appear to live entirely in water, and they have been known to follow a ship for miles in the disgusting hope of garbage being thrown to them by the steward. Their chief pastime is weighing each other, for which purpose they are liberally provided with scales. They can be captured by nets, or rods and lines, or, when they are cockles, they can be captured by the human hand, but, in this latter case, they cannot be tamed, having very little intelligence. he cockle has no scale, and feels the deprivation keenly, hiding himself deep in the sea and seldom venturing forth except at night-time. He is composed of two shells and a soft piece, is chiefly useful for poisoning children and is found at Sandymunt, a place where nobody but a cockle would live. Other fish may be generally described as, crabs, pinkeens, red herrings and whales. How these conduct their matrimonial adventures I do not know—the statement that whales are fond of pinkeens is true only in a food sense, for these races have never been observed to intermarry.

"A great many creatures capture or captivate their mates by singing.—These are usually, but not always, birds, and include wily wagtails, larks, canary birds and the crested earwig. Poets, music hall comedians and cats may also be included in this category. Dogs are imperative and dashing wooers, but they seldom sing. Peacocks expand their tails before the astonished gaze of their brides, showing how the female sex is over-borne by minor, unimportant advantages. Frogs, I believe, make love in the dark, which is a wise thing for them to do—they are very witty folk, but confirmed sentimentalists. Grocers' assistants attract their mates by exposing very tall collars and brown boots. Drapers' assistants follow suit, with the comely addition of green socks and an umbrella—they are never known to fail. Some creatures do not marry at all. At a certain period they break in two halves, and each half, fully equipped for existence, waggles away from the other.—They are the only perfectly happy folk of whom I am aware. For myself, I was born single and I will remain so, I will never be a slave to the disgusting habit of matrimony."

Having said this with great firmness, the old gentleman shed two more buttons from his waistcoat, and, after sticking three nails and a piece of twine through his garments, he departed very happily. The gentleman-in-waiting sneezed three times in a loud voice, and gave a war-whoop, but I took no notice of these impertinences.

I had not seen the old gentleman for a long time, and when he entered with one foot in a boot and the other in a carpet slipper, I was overjoyed. When the bubbling tankard which I had ordered was placed before him he seized my two hands, wrung them heartily and dashed into the following subject—

"It must be remembered," said he, "that dancing is not an art but a pastime, and should, therefore, be freed from the too-burdensome regulations wherewith an art is encumbered. An art is a highly-specialised matter hedged in on every side by intellectual policemen, a pastime is not specialised, and never takes place in the presence of policemen, who are well known to be the sworn enemies of gaiety. For example, theology is an art but religion is a pastime: we learn the collects only under compulsion, but we sing anthems because it is pleasant to do so. Thus, eating oysters is an art by dint of the elaborate ceremonial including shell-openers, lemons, waiters and pepper, which must be grouped around your oyster before you can conveniently swallow him, but eating nuts, or blackberries, or a privily-acquired turnip—these are pastimes.

"The practice of dancing is of an undoubted antiquity. History teems with reference to this custom, but it is difficult to discover what nationality or what era first witnessed its evolution. I myself believe that the first dance was performed by a domestic hen who found an ostrich's egg, and bounded before Providence in gratitude for something worthy of being sat upon.

"In all places and in all ages dancing has been utilised as a first-aid to language. The function of language is intellectual, that of dancing is emotional. It is scarcely possible to say anything of an emotional nature in words without adventuring into depths or bogs of sentimentality from which one can only emerge greasy with dishonour. When we are happy we cannot say so with any degree of intelligibility: in such a context the spoken word is miserably inadequate, and must be supplemented by some bodily antic. If we are merry we must skip to be understood. If we are happy we must dance. If we are wildly and ecstatically joyous then we will become creators, and some new and beneficent dance-movements will be added to the repertory of our neighborhood.

"Children will dance upon the slightest provocation, so also do lambs and goats; but policemen, and puckauns, and advertisement agents, and fish do not dance at all, and this is because they have hard hearts. Worms and Members of Parliament, between whom, in addition to their high general culture, there is a singular and subtle correspondence, do not dance, because the inelastic quality of their environment forbids anything in the nature of freedom. Frogs, dogs, and very young mountains do dance.

"A frog is a most estimable person. He has a cold body but a warm heart, and a countenance of almost parental benevolence, and the joy of life moves him to an almost ceaseless activity. I can never observe a frog on a journey without fancying that his gusto for travel is directed by a philanthropic impulse towards the bedside of a sick friend or a meeting to discuss the Housing of the Working Classes. He has danced all the way to, he will dance all the way from his objective, but the spectacle of many men dancing is provocative of pain.—To them dancing is a duty, and a melancholy one. If one danced to celebrate a toothache one might take lessons from them. They stand in the happy circle, their features are composed to an iron gravity, their hands are as rigid as those of a graven image, and then, the fatal moment having arrived, they agitate their legs with a cold fury which is distinctly unpleasant. Having finished they dash their partners from their sides and retire to blush and curse in a corner.

"When a man dances he should laugh and crow and snap his fingers and make faces; otherwise, he is not dancing at all, he is taking exercise. No person should be allowed to dance without first swearing that he feels only six years of age. People who admit to feeling more than ten years old should be sent to hospital, and any one proved guilty of fourteen years of age should be lodged in gaol without the option.

"It is peculiar how often opposite emotions may meet on a common plane of expression. The extremes of love and hate strive to get equally close to kiss or to bite the object of their regard. Work and play may be equally strenuous and equally enthralling. Hunger and satiety unite in a common boredom. A happy person will dance from sheer delight, and the man in whom a pin has been secreted can only by dancing express the exquisite sensibility of his cuticle. Whatever one does or refrains from doing one must be tired by bed-time—it is a law—but one may be pleasantly tired.

"I will suspect the morals of a man who cannot dance. I will look curiously into his sugar or statecraft. I will impeach his candour or reticence, and sneer at his method of lighting a fire unless he can frolic when he goes out for a walk with a dog— that is the beginning of dancing: the end of it is the beginning of a world. A young dog is a piece of early morning disguised in an earthly fell, and the man who can resist his contagion is a sour, dour, miserable mistake, without bravery, without virtue, without music, with a cranky body and a shrivelled soul, and with eyes incapable of seeing the sunlight.

"I have often thought that dogs are a very superior race of people. They are certainly more highly organised on the affectional plane than man. A dog will love you just for the fun of it—and that is virtue. Pat a dog on the head and he will dance around you in an ecstasy of good-fellowship. Let us, at least, be the equal of these sagacities. Let us put away our false intellectual pride. Let us learn to be unconscious. The average man trembles into a dance imagining that all eyes are rayed upon him wonderingly or admiringly, whereas, in truth, he will only be looked at if he dances very well or very badly. Both of these extremities of perfection ought to be avoided. We should exercise our very bad or very good qualities in solitude lest average people be saddened by their disabilities in either direction. Let your curses be as private as your prayers for both are purgative operations. In public we must conform to the standard, in private only may we do our best or our worst. Acting so, we will be freed from false pride and cowardly self-consciousness. Let us be brave. Let us caress the waists of our neighbours without fear. Let everybody's chin be our toy. Let us pat one another on the hats as we pass in the melancholy streets.—Thus only shall we learn to be gay and careless who for so long have been miserable and suspicious. We will be fearless and companionable who have been so timid and solitary. A new, a better, a real police force will arrest people who don't dance as they travel to and from their labour. The world will be happy at last, and civilisation will begin to be possible."

Here, in an ecstasy of good-fellowship, the old gentleman seized his pewter with his left hand and my glass with his right hand, and he emptied them both before recognising his mistake. I had, however, run out of tobacco, whereupon he became very angry, and refused to bid me good-night.

III

The old gentleman condescended to accept the last cigar which I had, and, having lit it with my only match, he earnestly advised me never to smoke to excess, because this indulgence brought spots before the eyes, deteriorated the moral character, and was, moreover, exceedingly expensive.—On the subject of smoking and tobacco he spoke as follows—

"I have observed that people who do not smoke are usually of a sour and unsociable disposition. All red-haired people smoke naturally, and they almost invariably use cut-plug. Very dark-haired men smoke twist, and their natural strength and virtue is such that in the intervals of smoking they also chew tobacco. Fair-haired men generally smoke cigarettes—they do this, not for the purpose of enjoyment, but purely in imitation of their betters. However, in later life, when they become bald, as they invariably do, they also became regenerate and smoke pig-tail. Men with mouse-coloured hair do not smoke at all. They collect postage stamps and sea-shells, and are usually to be found sitting round a fire with other girls eating chocolates and seeking for replies to such questions as, when is a door not a door? and why does a chicken cross the road? They are miserable creatures whom I will not further mention.

"The usage of tobacco, or some smokable substitute, is as old as primitive man. Almost all nations of the earth are adepts in this particular habit. It is, of course, an acquired taste, as also are washing and tomatoes. We are born with appetites which are static and unchangeable, but we are also born with a yearning for pleasure which is almost as positive as an appetite and only needs cultivation to become equally imperative. Doubtless, a traveller from some distant planet, who knew nothing of tobacco, would be astonished at the spectacle of a man exhaling smoke from his lips with splendid unconcern, and our traveller's conjectures as to the origin of the smoke and the immunity of the smoker would be highly amusing and instructive.

James Stephens

"I am often surprised on reflecting that our immediate ancestors were debarred from this pleasant indulgence, and I have wondered how they made the evenings pass. The lack of tobacco and pockets in their clothes (both of which are great civilising agents) may have been responsible for the wars, harryings, kidnappings and cattle raids which, alternating with rigorous and austere religious ceremonial, formed the bulk of their pleasures. Nowadays we leave these violent entertainments to children and the semi-literate and take our pleasures more composedly. A man who can put his hands in his pockets will seldom remove them for the purpose of slaying some one whose only fault is that he was born in the County Sligo. A man with a pipe in his teeth will be too much at peace with society to endanger its existence.

"If the blessings of tobacco should be extended to the remainder of the vertebrates (as, why should it not?) I am sure that lions, elephants, and wild boars would avail themselves of it. So, also, would kangaroos, a beautiful and agile race living in Polynesia, or thereabouts—they are beautiful hoppers, and collect large quantities of this plant. In this direction they are especially well equipped, each having a pouch in her stomach in which to carry tobacco and hops, but wherein they now ignorantly secrete their young. Serpents would smoke a pipe with considerable elegance, and might become more benevolent in consequence. Frogs would smoke, but I fancy they would expectorate too elaborately to be neighbourly. Fish, however, would not smoke at all.—They are a cowardly and corrupt people, living in water, which is a singular thing to do. Neither would many birds smoke, they have neither the stamina nor the teeth, but I am certain that crows and jackdaws would chew tobacco eagerly and with true relish. A large proportion of the insecta are too light-minded and frivolous to care for smoking. Beetles, however, a very reserved and dignified race, would smoke cigars, and so would cockroaches, a rather saturnine and cynical people; but no others.

"As for women—I am astonished they have not smoked, by

mere contagion, long ago. If they did they would certainly grow more kind-hearted and manly, and I am sure that a deputation of ladies with pipes in their mouths and hands in their pockets would only have to demand the franchise from an astounded ministry to obtain it.

"Members of Parliament are, I believe, either a separate creation or a composite of the parrot and the magpie. I have not yet discovered their particular function in nature but have observed them with some particularity. They wear top hats and are constantly making speeches, both of which are easy things to do and quite pleasant minor accomplishments.—So far as I can gather their chief use has been to pass something called a Budget. From the fact that this Budget contains a disgraceful imposition on tobacco I must take it that Members of Parliament are among the lower animals who do not smoke— they are also uninteresting in other ways."

Having said this my old friend bowed to me and departed genially with my cigar case in his pocket. The shirt-sleeved Adonis behind the counter wagged his head solemnly at a fly and then clouted it with a dish-cloth.

James Stephens

IV

The old gentleman took an athletic pull at his liquor, and continued his discourse. He had been discussing more to himself than to me the merits of Professor James and Monsieur Bergson, and had inquired was I aware of the nature of the Pragmatic Sanction. The gentleman behind the counter remarked, that he had one on his bicycle, but that they were no good. This statement was denounced by the Philosopher as an unnatural and clumsy falsehood, and, anathematising the ignorance of his interrupter, he came by slow degrees to the following discourse—

"I have but little faith in any of the methods of education with which I am presently acquainted. The objective of every system of teaching should be to enable the person who is being subjected to this repulsive treatment to do something which will fit him to maintain a place in life where he will be as little liable as possible to the changes and vicissitudes of civilised existence.

"The cumbrous and inadequate preparation which is now in vogue can scarcely be spoken of by a person of understanding without the use of language unbefitting one who is a member of (inter alia) the Reformed Church and the highest order of the vertebrates.

"If one walks into any school in this kingdom one is certain to meet a tall, thin, anaemic youth with a draggled moustache and a worried eye who is endeavouring to coerce a mass of indigestible, inelastic and unimportant facts into the heads of divers sleepy and disgusted children. If a small boy, on being asked where Labrador is, replies that it is the most northerly point of the Berlin Archipelago, he may be wrong in quite a variety of ways, but even if he answered correctly he would still know just as little about the matter, while if he were to give the only proper reply to so ridiculous a conundrum, he would tell his tormentor that he did not care a rap where it was, that he had not put it there, and that he would tell his mother if the man did not leave him alone. What has he got to do with Labrador, Terra del Fuego, or the Isles of Greece? Give him a fistful of facts about Donnybrook, and send him away to hunt out the truth of it, with a sandwich in his pocket and the promise of a lump of toffee when he came back with his cargo of truths—that would interest him, the toffee would make the information stick, while the verification of his facts would make his head fat and fertile.

"When we ceased to be natural creatures and put on the oppressive shrouds, wraps and disguises which we label in the villainous aggregate civilisation, we ceased to know either how to teach or how to learn. We exchanged the freedom and spaciousness of life for a cramped existence compounded of spectacles and bad grammar, this complicated still further by the multiplication tables, the dead languages and indigestion tabloids. During his school-days many a healthy boy had to parse ten square miles of dead language. Why? he does not know and he will never be told, for no one else knows any more than he. The only thing of which he is certain is, that he did not do anything to deserve it.

"Civilisation, which is responsible for all the woes of life, such as washing, shaving and buying boots, is responsible for this also. Potatoes are more productive than Latin roots, are twice as nourishing and cannot be parsed. Teach a girl how to recognise an egg by the naked eye, and then teach her how to cook it. Teach a boy how to discover the kind of trees eggs grow on and what is the best kind of soil to plant them in. Teach a girl how to keep her hands from scratching, her tongue from telling lies, and her teeth from dropping out prematurely, and she will, maybe, turn out a healthy kind of mammal having a house filled with brightness and laughter. Teach a boy how to prevent another boy from mashing the head off him, teach him how to be good to his mother when she is old, teach him how to give two-pence to a beggar without imagining that he is investing his savings in Paradise at fifty per cent and a bonus; and then, having eliminated

James Stephens

civilisation, education, clothes, tin whistles and soap this earth will not be such a bad old ball-alley for a man to smoke a pipe in.

"Everything is wrong. People should rise to their feet and salute when a farmer or a teacher comes into a room. No man should be allowed into Parliament who has not engaged in one or other of these professions, but because they are the two most important professions in the world their exponents are robbed and harried into slaves and fools."

Having said this with great earnestness the old gentleman absent-mindedly impounded my drink, absorbed it, and strode away wrapped in thought. The gentleman-in-waiting sympathetically asked me if I would have another one, but on learning that I had no more money he said good-night.

V

The old gentleman was in a state of most unusual content. It might have been because the sun was shining, or it might have been because he had just finished his third glass: whatever it was, the smile upon his face was of a depth and a radiance impossible to describe. He spoke for a while upon the pleasant smell of hay passing through a city, and, remarking upon the enviable thirst of hay-makers, he swept gradually to the following weighty monologue—

"From the earliest times," said he, "drinking has been regarded not alone as a necessary lubricant, but also as a pastime, and the ingenuity of every race under the sun has been exercised in the attempt to give variety and distinction to its beverages.

"We may take it that the earliest race of men drank nothing but water, and hot water to boot, for at that era the earth must have been, if not hot, at least tepid. One can easily imagine that the contemporaries of the five-toed horse might have welcomed death as a happy release from their too sultry existence.

"I suppose man is the only brewing animal known to scientific research. All other creatures take their food and drink neat, or in a raw state. Of course, almost all mammals are enabled by a highly ingenious internal mechanism to brew milk, or some other lacteal substitute, but this is performed by a natural, instinctive impulse towards the preservation of their young and conserves none of the spirit of artifice and calculation so necessary to authentic brewing operations.

"Brewing was possible only when the stability of the human race was, more or less, assured and permanent. Our primal ancestors existed in a state as nearly resembling chaos as well might be. They had not yet aggregated into communities, but vast hordes of families—a father, an uncertain number of mothers, and an astounding complexity

James Stephens

of children—wandered wherever food seemed most abundant, and fought with or eluded such other families as they chanced upon. This state of existence was too precarious and haphazard to allow of the niceties of brewing being evolved.

"But the natural tendency of families to lengthen, the gregarious instincts of the race, and the need of mutual protection and assistance ultimately welded these indiscriminate families into communities of ever-varying extent, and the movement of these huge troops and transportation of their baggage becoming more and more difficult (vehicles being unknown and horses, perhaps, treble-toed, wily and ferocious) and food, which until then had only been obtained in a fugitive state, becoming less easy of access, these communities were forced to select a settled habitation, scratch the earth for provender, settled down to the breeding of one-toed horses, and exercise the respectable virtues of thrift and industry for their preservation. Thus, laws were formulated, tentative and unsatisfactory at first, and ever tending, as to this day, to become more complex and less satisfactory. Villages took shape, straggled into towns, widened into cities and coalesced into kingdoms and empires: and so, the civilisation of which we are partakers crawled laboriously into being, with the brewer somewhere in the centre, active, rubicund and disputatious, as he has continued to date, with a seat on the County Council which he had swindled some thirsty statesman out of, and more property than he could deal with by himself.

"It is a singular reflection that thirst has very little to do with the consumption of drink, nor is this appetite subject to the vagaries of climate, for the inhabitants of the coldest regions will, it is feared, drink on equal terms with those dwelling in the sun-burnt tropics. In almost all ceremonial observances drinking has had a special place, and this diversion lends itself to an infinite number of objects—we can from the same bowl quaff health to our friends and confusion to our enemies, doubtless with equal results. Here alone men meet on equal terms. There is no religion, nationality or politics in liquor: let it be but sufficiently wet and potent and it matters not if the brew has been fermented in the tub of a Christian or the vessel of a heathen Turk.

"I understand that this latter race are forbidden, by the form of heresy which they call religion, to use liquors more potent than sherbet. Some thinkers believe that this deprivation is possibly the reason of their being Turks.—They are Turks, not from conviction, but from habit, spite, and the bile engendered by a too rigid and bigoted abstinence. In this belief, however, I do not concur, for I consider that a Turk is a Turk naturally, and without any further constraint than those imposed by the laws of geography and primogeniture.

"Meanwhile it is interesting to speculate on the future of an abstinent nation whose politics have the misfortune to be guided by a Peerage instead of a Beerage, and whose national destiny is irrationally divorced from the interests of 'The Trade.' Any departure from the established customs of humanity must be criticised unsparingly, and, if necessary, destructively. To overthrow the customs of antiquity must entail its own punishment and that punishment may be an awe-inspiring and chastening Success. Therefore, this happy whisky-governed land of ours should never forsake its liquor or it may be forced by opportunity and work to become great. The foundations of our civilisation are steeped in beer—let no sacrilegious hand seek to interfere with it, for, even if the foundations were rotten, the interests of the Trade must not be disturbed, the grave and learned members of our Corporation might be horribly reduced to working for their living, and our unfortunate City might have the extraordinary misfortune to scramble out of debt in the absence of its statesmen."

The old gentleman, with a bright smile, said that "he did not mind if he did," and he "did" with such gusto that I had to call a cab.

VI

The old gentleman came in hurriedly and called for that to which he was accustomed. He fumbled in one pocket after another, and after going over all his pockets several times he remarked to me "I have forgotten my purse." His air was so friendly and confiding that it more than repaid me for the small sum which I had to advance. He sat down close beside me, and, after touching on the difficulty of being understood in a tavern, he drew genially to these remarks—

"Language may be described as a medium for recording one's sensations. It is gesture translated into sound. It is noise with a meaning. Music cannot at all compare with it, for music is no more than the scientific distribution of noise, and it does not impart any meaning to the disintegrated and harried tumults. Language may be divided into several heads, which, again, may be subdivided almost indefinitely.—The primary heads are, language, talk, and speech. Speech is the particular form of noise which is made by Members of Parliament. Language is the symbols whereby one lady in a back street makes audible her impressions of the lady who lives on the same floor—it is often extremely sinewy. Talk may be described as the crime of people who make one tired.

"It is my opinion that people talk too much. I think the world would be a healthier and better place if it were more silent. On every day that passes there is registered over all the earth a vast amount of language which, so far as I can see, has not the slightest bearing on anything anywhere.

"I have been told of a race living in Central Africa, or elsewhere, who by an inherent culture were enabled to dispense with speech. They whistled, and by practice had attained so copious and flexible a vocabulary that they could whistle good-morning and good-night, or how-do-you-do with equal facility and distinction. This, while it is a step in the right direction, is not a sufficiently long step. To live among these people might appear very like living in a cageful of canaries or parrots. Parrots are a very superior race who usually travel with sailors. They have a whistle which can be guided or deflected into various by-ways. I once knew a parrot who was employed by a sailor-man to curse for him when his own speech was suspended by liquor. He could also whistle ballads and polkas, and had attained an astonishing proficiency in these arts; for, by long practice, he could dovetail curses and whistles in a most energetic and, indeed, astonishing manner. It would often project two whistles and a curse, sometimes two curses and a whistle, while all the time keeping faithfully to the tune of 'The Sailor's Grave' or another. It was a highly cultivated and erudite person. As it advanced in learning it took naturally to chewing tobacco, but, being a person of strongly experimental habits, it tried one day to curse and whistle and chew tobacco at the one moment, with the unfortunate result that a piece of honeydew got jammed between a whistle and a curse, and the poor thing perished miserably of strangulation.

"It is indeed singular that while every race of mankind is competent to speak, none of the other races, such as cats, cows, caterpillars, and crabs, have shown the slightest interest in the making of this ordered noise. This is the more strange when we reflect that almost all animals are provided with a throat and a mouth which are capable of making a noise certainly equal in volume and intelligibility to the sounds made by a German or a Spaniard.

"Long ago men lived in trees and had elongated backbones which they were able to twitch. There were no shops, theatres, or churches in those times, and, consequently, no necessity for a specialized and meticulous prosody. Man barked at his fellow-man when he wanted something, and if his request was not understood he bit his fellow-man and was quit of him. When they forsook the trees and became ground-walkers they came into contact with a variety of theretofore unknown objects, the necessity for naming which so exercised their tongues that gradually their bark took on a different quality and became susceptible of more complicated sounds. Then, with the dawning of the Pastoral Age, food in a gregarious community became a matter of more especial importance. When a man barked at his wife for a cocoanut and she handed him a baby or a bowl of soup or an evening paper it became necessary, in order to minimise her alternatives, that he should elaborate his bark to meet this and an hundred other circumstances. I do not know at what period of history man was able to call his wife names with the certainty of reprisal. It was possible quite early, because I have often heard a dog bark in a dissatisfied and important manner at another dog and be perfectly comprehended.

"A difficulty would certainly arise as to the selection of a word when forty or fifty men might at the same time label any article with as many different names, and, it is reasonable to suppose, that they would be reluctant to adopt any other expression but that of their own creation. In such a crux the strongest man of the community would be likely to clout the others to an admission that his terminology was standard.

"Thus, by slow accretions, the various languages crept into currency, and the youth of innumerable schoolboys has been embittered by having to learn to spell.

"Grasshoppers are a fine, sturdy race of people. A great many of them live on the Hill of Howth, where I have often spent hours hearkening to their charming conversation. They do not speak with the same machinery that we use—they convey their ideas to each other by rubbing their hind-legs together, whereupon noises are produced of exceeding variety and interest. As a method of speech this is simply delightful, and I wish we could be trained to converse in so majestical a manner. Perhaps we shall live to see the day when the journals will chronicle that Mr. Redmond had rubbed his legs together for three hours at the Treasury Bench and was removed frothing at the feet, but after a little rest he was enabled to return and make more noise than ever."

The old gentleman smiled very genially and went out. The assistant suggested that he had a terrible lot of old "guff," but I did not agree with him.

James Stephens

VII

Between impartial sips at his own and my liquor the old gentleman perused the small volume which he had taken from my pocket. After he had read it he buttoned the book in his own pouch and addressed me with great kindness—

"In some respects," said he, "poets differ materially from other animals. For instance, they seldom marry, and when they do it is only under extreme compulsion.—This is the more singular when we remember that poets are almost continually singing about love. When they do marry they instantly cease to make poetry and turn to labour like the rest of the community.

"It has been finely said that the poet is born and not made, but I fancy that this might be postulated of the rest of creation.

"Many people believe that all poets arise from their beds in the middle of the night, and that they walk ten miles until they come to a hillside, where they remain until the dawn whistling to the little birds; but this, while it is true in some instances, is not invariably true. A proper poet would not walk ten miles for any one except a publisher.

"The art of writing poetry is very difficult at first, but it becomes easy by practice. The best way for a beginner is to take a line from another poem; then he should construct a line to fit it; then, having won his start, he should strike out the first line (which, of course, does not belong to him) and go ahead. When the poet has written three verses of four lines each he should run out and find a girl somewhere and read it to her. Girls are always delighted when this is done. They usually clasp their hands together as though in pain, roll their eyes in an ecstasy, and shout, 'How perfectly perfect!' Then the poet will grip both her hands very tightly and say he loves her but will not marry her, and, in an agony of inspiration, he will tear himself away and stand drinks to himself until he is put out. This is, of course, only one way of being a poet. If he perseveres he will ultimately write lyrics for the music halls and make a fortune. He will then wear a fur coat that died of the mange, he will support a carnation in his buttonhole, wear eighteen rings on his right hand and one hundred and twenty-seven on his left. He will also be entitled to wear two breast-pins at once and yellow boots. He will live in England when he is at home, and be very friendly with duchesses.

"Poetry is the oldest of the arts. Indeed, it may be called the parent of the arts. Poetry, music, and dancing are the only relics which have come down to us from those ancient times which are termed impartially the Golden or the Arboreal Ages. In ancient Ireland the part played by the poet was very important. Not alone was he the singer of songs, he was also the bestower of fame and the keeper of genealogies, and, therefore, he was treated with a dignity which he has since refused to forget. When a poet made a song in public, it was customary that the king and the nobility should divest themselves of their jewels, gold chains, and rings, and give this light plunder to him. They also bestowed on him goblets of gold and silver, herds of cattle, farms, and maidservants. The poets are not at all happy in these constricted times, and will proclaim their astonishment and repugnance in the roundest language.

"A few days ago I was speaking in Grafton Street to a poet of great eminence, and, with tears in his voice, he told me that he had never been offered as much as a bracelet by any lady. Times have changed; but for the person who still wishes to enter this decayed profession there is still every opportunity, for poetry is only the art of cutting sentences into equal lengths, and then getting these sentences printed by a publisher. It is in the latter part of this formula that the real art consists.

"There are a great many poets in Ireland, particularly in Dublin. In an evening's walk one may meet at least a dozen of this peculiar people. They may be known by the fact that they wear large, soft hats, and that the breast-pockets of their coats have a more than noticeable bulge, due to their habit of carrying therein the twenty-seven masterpieces which they have just written. They are very ethereal creatures, composed largely of soul and thirst. Soul is a far-away, eerie thing, generally produced by eating fish."

The old gentleman borrowed the price of a tram home; but as he instantly stood himself a drink with it, I was forced to relend him the money when we got outside.

VIII

The old gentleman was in a very bad temper when I arrived. He had a large glass of porter in his hand—a pint, in fact—and he was gazing on this liquid with no great favour. I was a little surprised at his choice of a drink, for I had never before known him care for any other refreshment than spirits; but I did not like to make any reference to the change. Looking thus, with great disgust, upon his pint, he began to talk with some asperity about the English nation.

"The ways of Providence," said he, "are indeed inscrutable, else why should there be such things in the world as lobsters, gutta-percha, ballet-dancers, and Englishmen? These four objects, and some others—notably water, tram-cars, and warts—I can find no necessity for in nature; but there must be some reason for such, or else they could not have arrived at the more or less mature stage of development at which they are found.

"If we apply the canons of the Pragmatic philosophy to these objects we will arrive at some conclusion which, although it may not justify their existence, will give a hint as to their expediency. The question to be put to any doubtful fact in nature is this—'What is your use?' and the reality of the fact is in ratio to the degree of usefulness inhering in it. Thus treated, most of the objects to which I have referred may be able to adduce some excuse for their existence. A lobster may aver that if he were not alive his absence would be a severe blow to the lobster-pot industry, and would throw many respectable families on the already-overburdened rates. Gutta-percha might plead that it has aspired through many millions of ages to a maturity which would enable it to rub out lead-pencil marks. Ballet-dancers would have a great deal to say for themselves, possibly on moral grounds; but I really see no reason for Englishmen.

"I have said that an object is real in ratio to its usefulness. If we examine an Englishman thus pragmatically we must discover that his usefulness is zero, and we are then forced to inquire why he exists at all, for he does undoubtedly exist, as witness this pint of porter which I hold in my hand, and which I do hold in my hand solely on account of the unexplainable existence of Englishmen. "I may say at once that I never indulge in this particular form of refreshment, against which I have nothing further to charge than it does not agree with my system, but I am no bigot in such matters, and can quite willingly believe that lower natures and less cultivated palates may take pleasure in secreting this inordinately lengthy liquid. I cannot avoid the belief that any liquid which may be imbibed by the imperial pint is an essentially gross drink, and one unfitted for persons of a high culture. Nor can I find in nature that any of the more specialised organisms take their drink in such extravagant quantities. Camels, who, I am informed, are a very well-behaved and moral race leading rigorous and chaste lives in a desert, do drink deeply, but their excess is more apparent than real, for Providence in an aberration endowed these folk with more stomachs than the average person possesses, and the necessity for filling these additional cisterns accounts for and justifies their liberal use of moisture. Worms, on the other hand, are a folk for whom I have very little reverence and no affection. I am not aware whether they are all stomach or all neck, but from their corner-boy expression I am inclined to fancy that worms would drink pints if they could. Happily, this disgusting exhibition is forbidden by the imperfect state of their civilisation and the inelastic quality of their environment.

"But this is beside the point. My grievance is, that in my old age I am forced to drink porter which disagrees with my liver, and am compelled to abstain from spirits which have a sustaining and medicinal effect on that organ, and this deprivation is solely due to the unnatural and inexplicable existence of Englishmen. It may be that nature grew Englishmen for the sole purpose of interfering with my organs, and so, by modifying my teaching in accordance with my diseased interior, nature may be striving to evolve a new culture wherein bile will have a rare ability. If this is so, then I am not at all obliged to nature for singling me out as the instrument of her changes; if it is not so I can only confess my ignorance and wash my hands of the matter.

"Mark you, it was only during my lifetime that an exorbitant tax was placed on whisky. Before my era the interference with this refreshment was of the most tentative and apologetic description.

"I can remember, and I do remember with dismay, the time when whisky was purchaseable at two bronze pennies for the naggin, but now one may discharge a ruinous impost for the privilege of imbibing one poor fourth of that happy measure.

"This has been brought about by the continuous interference of Englishmen with my liquor. Time and again they have added additional difficulties to my obtaining this medicinal refreshment, and, while I am compelled to bow my head to the ideas of nature for the improvement of our race, I am often inclined, having bowed it, to charge goat-like at these intolerable people and butt them off the face of the earth into the nowhere for which their villainous and ungenial habits have fitted them. Otherwise, by their future exactions I may be brought to the drinking of benzene or printer's ink for lack of a fortune wherewith to purchase fitter refreshment."

Having said this with great fury, the old gentleman laid down his untasted pint and stalked out. The acolyte behind the counter made a sympathetic clicking noise with his tongue and sold the pint to another man.—He probably did this thoughtlessly, and I did not care to embarrass him by remarking on it.

IX

I met the old gentleman marching solemnly across Cork Hill. There was a tramcar in his immediate rear, a cab in front of him, an outside-car and a bicycle on his right hand, and a dray laden with barrels on his left. The drivers of all these vehicles were entreating him in one voice to stroll elsewhere. He looked around and, observing that matters were complicated, he opened his umbrella, held it over his head, and awaited events with the most admirable fortitude. When I had escorted him to the pavement, and further to his own hostelry, he seized the third button of my waistcoat and spake as follows:—

"It is an admirable example of the wisdom of nature that she has refrained in every case from equipping her creatures with wheels instead of legs, and she might easily have done this. So far as I am aware there are but four methods of progression in nature—these are, flying, swimming, walking and crawling. None of these are performed with a rotary motion, and all are admirably adapted to the people using them, and are sufficiently expeditious to suit their needs.

"There is no doubt that the most primitive of movements is that of crawling, and by this method of progression, one is brought into an intimate contact with the earth which cannot fail to be beneficial. I do not see any real difficulty in the way of our again becoming a race of happy and crawling people. The initial essay towards this end is to shed our arms and legs as useless incumbrances, and then to aim at a stronger growth of jaw and cranium. Among certain organisms it will be found that the jaws are the most immediately useful parts of the body, performing the most varied and delicate functions with the greatest ease. A dog, for example, will, with the one organ, play with a ball, kill a cat, or nip the calf of a Christian, and, when the moon is high, he can make a noise with his mouth which is as loud and quite as melodious as the professional clamour of a ballad-vocalist.

"One of the greatest evils of civilisation is the longing for speed, which, within the past hundred years, has developed from a simple vice to a complicated mania. Long ago men were accustomed to use their legs in order to propel themselves forward, and, when greater speed was necessary, they assisted their legs with their hands—this was coeval with, or shortly after, the arboreal age. Next came the hunting epoch, when some person, probably a commercial traveller, dropped off a tree on to a horse's back, and finding the movement pleasant he informed his companions of his adventure and demonstrated to them how it had been performed. It is from this occurrence we may date the degradation of the human race and the industry of horse-stealing. There followed the pastoral age, when nuts were, more or less, abandoned as a food and tillage became general. The necessity for conveying the crops from the field to the camp excited some lazy individual to invent a cart, and, thus, wheels came into use and the doom of humanity as an instinctive and natural race was sealed.

"While we walked on our own legs we were natural and instinctive creatures, open to every impression of nature and able to tell the time without clocks, but when we adopted mechanical methods of progression we became unnatural and mechanical people, whizzing restlessly and recklessly from here to yonder, for no purpose save the mere sensual pleasure of movement, and we are at this date simply debauched by travel and have shortened the world to less than one-tenth of its actual size as well as destroying our abilities for simple and rational enjoyment.

"If we continue using these artificial means of locomotion there is no doubt that the race will become atrophied in the legs but with extraordinary results. The spectacle of an egg-shaped humanity squatting painfully on engines is not a pleasant one to contemplate, nor is the prospect of a world wherein there will be neither breeches nor boots good for the moralist or economist to dwell upon.

"In order to conserve the happiness of the world every inventor should be squashed in the egg, more particularly those having anything to do with wheels, cogs or levers. The wheel has no counterpart in nature, and is unthinkable to any but a diseased and curious mind. Man will never more be happy until he has broken all the machinery he can find with a hammer, and has then thrown the hammer into the sea; and then he can, by experiment, become almost as rooted in the earth as a tree or an artesian well. It is a bad thing to have an indefinite horizon. It is a good thing to grow knowing one part of the world as thoroughly as one knows the inside of one's boots. Legs make for nationality, patriotism, and all the virtues which centre in locality. Wheels make for diffuseness, imperialisms, cosmo-politanisms. By the use of legs humanity has stalked into manhood. By the use of wheels we are rapidly rolling into a race of commercial travellers, touts, gad-abouts, and members of parliament, folk with the hanging jaws of astonishment, avid for curios, and with mental, moral and optical indigestion.

"I believe that the Spanyols and Mandibaloes, two Mongol races inhabiting the countries at the rear of the Great Chow Desert, were the first people to deal largely with wheels. The men of these nations were used, when travelling, to affix two small wheels upon their shoulder blades, and on coming to any slight incline in their path they would curl up their legs, lie on their backs and free-wheel as distantly as the slant of the ground permitted, greatly, no doubt, to the astonishment of less sophisticated people. But, knowing their habits, their enemies were wont to lie in wait at the bottoms of hills and slopes, and when a Spanyol or Mandibaloe came wheeling down a hill with his legs up he was killed before he could regain a less complicated position, or one more fitted for defence or offence. Thus, these races became rapidly extinct, and are now only remembered by the tracks as wide as a man's shoulderblades which are occasionally found in parts of the post-tertiary formation."

The old gentleman released the third button of my waistcoat

which he had held for so long and stepped with me out of the hostel. As it had begun to rain he carefully folded up his umbrella, tucked it under his arm, and strode rapidly down the street. Some small boys followed him for a little time singing, "We are the boys of Wexford who fought with heart and hand," but I drove these away.

James Stephens

X

He wiped his face with a large, red pocket-handkerchief, pursed his lips, shut one eye, and, with the other, he critically observed the remnant of his liquor. After a moment of deep consideration he smiled delightfully and said he thought it was all right. The apothecary behind the counter smiled also as one gratified and suggested that there was not much of that at the North Pole, and, after a little discussion on this point, the old gentleman addressed me in the following words:—

"I do not understand what necessity impels people to the discovery of something, which, if it has any existence at all, has only an idealistic existence, and which, when it is discovered, cannot be utilised in any possible direction. Utility is the first attribute of all terrestrial bodies. A stone, for instance, is a useful inorganic substance—it can be built into a house, or thrown at a duck, or, when ground into sand, it can be, and is, sold as sugar by a grocer. It is constantly being utilised in one or other of these directions; and so with all other objects. But the necessity for a North or a South Pole has yet to be demonstrated. "The statement that the North Pole was put there by the Castle authorities is one which I do not believe, for I am assured that at every period of the world's history there has been a North and a South Pole, which, surrounded as they were by snow-clad countries, icebergs, cold water and whales, were too remote and inhospitable to tempt the average civilian to journey there.

"The only thing which grows in the Polar regions is ice, and this is generally found in almost tropical profusion and rankness, growing sometimes to the height of several hundred feet, none of which wear boots. Polar bears and Esquimos are also found there, but in scattered and inconsiderable quantities. These two races spend most of their time chasing each other in order to keep themselves warm, which they do by degrees which are often registered on a barometer. They also eat each other and get scurvy. Outside of these relaxations their existence is stagnant and unexciting. I sometimes fancy that if I had the misfortune to be born a polar bear or an Esquimo I would not have been a patriot.

"I have no esteem for ice in other than easily portable quantities. Some small pieces to pack around fish, a particle to drop into a glass of lager beer—that is all the ice which I can regard patiently or leniently; but a continent composed entirely of ice and polar bears tempts me to believe that Providence is subject to aberrations.

"It is supposed to redound to the credit of a nation when one of its citizens resolves to discover some inaccessible and futile place, and proceeds to do so in the most fantastic manner. The inhabitants of that country who remain at their work and continue to pay their rates are expected to be in a condition of wild enthusiasm and delight at the adventure.—My own impression is, that the majority of people take no more than a tepid interest in these forlorn adventures, and are but imperfectly convinced of the sanity of the adventurers; and this is the more particularly noticeable when the quest is for something so intangible and unmarketable as a North Pole. Why need they go so far afield for their excitement? Every discoverer is a detective. He traces missing places, and there are cartloads of Poles in their own countries waiting for explorers.

"The habit of seeking for a North Pole is one of only comparative antiquity. Its conception is well within the historic era, and must, therefore, be classed as an acquired habit and one not inherent in man. I have not observed that any other animals are addicted to this peculiar expeditionary craze. It is true that many species of birds migrate annually from these shores, and, although their departures are usually chronicled in the newspapers, it must not without further evidence be inferred that these birds have gone to look for the North Pole. They may, as a matter of fact, have left this country to avoid being arrested, for here one is continually being arrested. The evidence in favour of the North Pole theory as regards birds is, that nobody knows where they have gone to, and that as the rest of the earth is round and densely populated their arrival would be noted somewhere as their departure was, but their arrival not being so noted, and as they must be somewhere, the process of eliminating all possible places leaves nowhere but the North Pole as their objective. Now birds are a very intelligent and strenuous race of people who build nests in trees and have often five eggs at a time, and I believe that they leave these countries because their nests are full of broken egg-shells, and because the winter is setting in, and because they dislike cold weather; and, thus disliking cold weather, it is unlikely that they would fly to the North Pole where the cold is very intense, and where, moreover, there is little food to be found, saving polar bears and Esquimos, a form of victual for which birds have only the scantiest relish. My own impression is, that these birds when out of sight of land are enabled by a mechanism with which we are not yet familiar, to convert themselves into fishes, or, alternatively, that they know the whereabouts of Tir na n-Og and go there, or else that they do not go anywhere at all but are simply translated into the Fourth Dimension of Space, and are, thus, flying, nesting and mating all around us in a medium which our eyes are too gross to penetrate.

"From a perusal of the evening papers I observe that the discoverer of the North Pole is an American citizen with a complicated pedigree, a long beard and a red shirt, all of which he hoisted to the top of the Pole and left there for subsequent identification. I fear this was a thoughtless action on his part because the Esquimos who live habitually at the North Pole, but have not discovered it, will, while his back is turned, take to wearing his shirt in turn. They are a communistic people, I fancy, and no shirt will survive communism. Also, seeing the fuss which is being made of their Pole, they may either hide it or sell pieces of it to tourists as remembrancers.

"The explorer should have cached his shirt and other memorials at the foot of the Pole, built a cairn upon it, and shook cayenne pepper on top of all to keep bears away—but it is useless to advise explorers."

The ancient hereupon made a significant gesture to the curate, who misinterpreted it, and brought more than he had required. He was very much perturbed, for, as he explained, he had forgotten to bring his purse with him. He consented, however, to use my purse for his needs, and, after paying his shot, he, in an abstracted and melancholy manner, put the change in his trouser pocket. There was only one shilling in the purse so I did not like to draw his attention to the mistake. He very genially returned my purse, and said he had conceived a great liking for me.

XI

When the old gentleman came in I noticed at once that he was out of humour. He had a large scar on his chin, and three pieces of newspaper on his cheeks. He discharged the contents of my tobacco pouch into a pipe which had a holding capacity of one and a half ounces, and then he became more cheerful—

"I dislike extremely," said he, "the impertinent interference with nature which men are nowadays guilty of. Not content with clamping our feet in leathern boxes, our legs in cloth cylinders, our trunks in a variety of wrappings of complex inutility, and then inserting our heads into monstrous felt pots, we even approach ourselves more minutely and scrape the very hair from our faces which nature has sown there for purposes of ornament and protection; with the result, that it is difficult for a short-sighted person to distinguish rapidly the sex of the people with whom he comes in contact saving by a minute and tedious examination of their clothing.

"This habit of shaving is one which is entirely confined to man. It is the one particular habit that he holds apart from all other animals, and, indeed, it is not an accomplishment upon which he need pride himself, for in parting with his beard he has sacrificed the only pleasant-looking portion of his face.

"It could easily be proved that hair and innocence have a subtle relationship. No very hairy person is really vicious, as witness the caterpillar, of whom I have not heard that he ever bit any one: while, on the other hand, the frog, who is born bald, would doubtless be very savage were it not for the fact that nature has benevolently curtailed his teeth. Fishes, also, an uncleanly race, and who I fancy are shaved before birth, are all monsters of cold-blooded ferocity, and they will devour their parents and even their own offspring with equal and indiscriminate enjoyment.

"The habit of shaving is not of a very ancient origin. When

humanity lived a quiet, rural and unambitious life, men did not shave: their hair was their glory, and if they had occasion to swear, which must have been infrequent, their hardiest and readiest oath was, 'by the beard of my father,' showing clearly that this texture was held in veneration in early times and was probably accorded divine honours upon suitable occasions.

"With the advent of war came the habit of shaving. A beard offered too handy a grip to a foeman who had gotten to close quarters, therefore, warriors who had no true hardihood of soul preferred cutting off their beards to the honourable labour of defending their chins. Many ancient races effected a compromise in order to retain a fitting military appearance, for a bare-faced warrior has but little of terror in his aspect. The ancient Egyptians, for example, who had cut off, or could not cultivate, or had been forcibly deprived of their beards, were wont to go into battle clad in heavy false whiskers, which, when an enemy seized hold of them, came off instantly in his hand, and the ancient Egyptian was enabled to despatch him while in a trance of stupefaction and horror. Clean-shaved men became, by this cowardly stratagem, very much prized as fighting men, and thus the foundation of the shaving habit was laid.

"It is a remarkable fact that, save for an inconsiderable number who live in circuses, women have no beards. I am unable at present to trace the reason for this singular omission, but the advantages of beards for women are too patent for explanation. They would improve her personal appearance, and their advantages as air-purifiers or respirators I need not dwell upon. I am certain that a persistent application of goose-grease and electricity to the chin of a woman would at last enable her to become as bearded and virtuous as her husband, besides entitling her to the political franchise. They are perverse creatures, however, and it is possible that this deprivation is responsible for many of their ill-humours and crankinesses. Their scarcity of beard is the more remarkable when we observe that the female cat is as magnificently whiskered as her male companion. The wisdom of cats is proverbial, and I have never heard of a cat who has hired another cat to bite out, tear off, scrape or otherwise demolish his or her whiskers. When I do hear of some such occurrence I shall be prepared to reconsider my position on this subject.

"In some ways a clean-shaved face is desirable. A pig's cheek should not have whiskers, neither should oysters nor the face of a clock, but a man's face should never be seen out of doors without a decent and honourable covering."

Having said this, the old gentleman, with remarkable presence of mind, drank my whisky, and then apologised with dignified and touching humility. As we departed the youth behind the counter corrugated his features in a remarkable manner, and said, "bow-wow" by way of valediction.

XII

He helped himself absently to two water biscuits and a piece of cheese and sank to a profound reverie. The eating of this light refreshment was probably a manifestation of subconscious thought, for, when he had finished, he spoke to me as follows—

"There are a great many things which I dislike immensely but the necessity for which I must perforce acquiesce in: these are water, easterly winds and actresses: but there are other habits cultivated by humanity for which I can find no apology, and some of these have grown to so great an extent that they now bulk as evils of terrific magnitude."

"Foremost among these reprehensible customs I will mention that of eating. Of all the evils under which civilisation staggers helplessly the most ponderous and merciless is hunger, and it is the evil which will ultimately decimate all existing forms of life.

"All forms of organic life have now for millions of years been slaves to this filthy habit of eating, and have superimposed upon their original singleness of form a variety of weighty and unattractive organs to keep pace with the satisfaction of this oppressive appetite, until to-day the entire organic world stands upon the imminent brink of destruction if food should be withheld from it for one entire week.

"Every living being should be self-supporting and self-sufficient. It should be inherent in the economy of a man to produce for himself not alone food but also shelter and raiment from his own internal resources. A man should be able to build a house or evolve a loaf of bread out of his own body with ease and assurance.

"Look for a moment at spiders. Every spider carries within himself the materials for his own home. His stomach, instead

James Stephens

of being, as is vulgarly supposed, a cemetery for smaller organisms, is in reality his brick-field and rope-walk, and out of this minute sack he will produce endless miles of cordage and web which he weaves into the most beautiful and mathematical harmonies. This is a self-contained utility which might be imitated by men with advantage, and that which is done with ease by a spider can scarcely offer insuperable difficulty to the chief of the vertebrates. Of course, each man's production will be more or less guided and limited by his capacity.—Thus, fat men will spin forth cathedrals, opera-houses and railway stations. Thin men will devote themselves to obelisks, church spires, factory chimneys, and artistic bric-a-brac. Short men will willingly produce artisans' dwellings, busts of famous men and, perhaps, now and then, pyramids or villa residences. Constant work of this description will not alone render us independent of landlords, but, by atrophy of the digestive organs, will inaugurate a brighter era for long-suffering, food-fed humanity.

"Suppose it is advanced that man cannot keep up his strength and usefulness without some kind of exterior nourishment—I will then proceed to demonstrate how this can be most easily accomplished. Our first cousins, the trees and bushes, do not sit down at stated hours to a heterogeneous mess of steak, tea and onions: they stand firm in the ground unhurried by the sound of the dinner-bell and careless of the state of the American market. As the spider is sufficient in itself in house-building, so are the trees, the grass and all inorganic life self-supporting so far as food is concerned. The reason is, that trees, grass and flowers are bedded in the earth, the source of all nourishment. Let this fact be but properly understood, and the last and greatest bar to human progress will be removed, and 'the millenniums which so furiously chase us' will have a chance of catching us up.

"If, once a week, men would bury themselves to the chin in good fertile clay, and allow the nurture of the earth to permeate their bodies there would be an end to this gross and unfortunate digestive activity. I have myself experimented in this direction with the most encouraging results. A rich, loamy soil is very good—it is rather cold at the bottom, but invigorating. Light, sandy clay would suit sedentary persons such as parsons, artists, judges. In poor ground some superphosphates, or a light compost could be strewn by each person around himself. Families would take turns in pruning each other, and so forth; but all these incidental matters would rapidly adjust themselves. After a time we might succeed in propagating ourselves by seeds or slips, and this would lead to a radical readjustment of our sex relations and put an end to many of the problems herewith we are eternally badgered and perplexed.

"In some ways I will admit that food is valuable. As a means of killing a rich uncle by gout, or of attaining wealth by judicious adulteration it can be recommended, and looked at in the light of a gentle morning exercise to be taken immediately after rising it is useful, but as a method of obtaining nourishment it is obsolete and disgustingly vulgar."

At this point the gentleman-in-waiting snorted in a most unbecoming manner, and dived under the counter, from beneath which he alternately mewed like a cat and crowed like a cock. It was a clear attack of hysteria. While the poor man was recovering from his seizure the old gentleman absent-mindedly departed without paying his shot.

THE END

James Stephens

Choose from Thousands of 1stWorldLibrary Classics By

A. M. Barnard	Booth Tarkington	Edward Everett Hale
Ada Leverson	Boyd Cable	Edward J. O'Biren
Adolphus William Ward	Bram Stoker	Edward S. Ellis
Aesop	C. Collodi	Edwin L. Arnold
Agatha Christie	C. E. Orr	Eleanor Atkins
Alexander Aaronsohn	C. M. Ingleby	Eleanor Hallowell Abbott
Alexander Kielland	Carolyn Wells	Eliot Gregory
Alexandre Dumas	Catherine Parr Traill	Elizabeth Gaskell
Alfred Gatty	Charles A. Eastman	Elizabeth McCracken
Alfred Ollivant	Charles Amory Beach	Elizabeth Von Arnim
Alice Duer Miller	Charles Dickens	Ellem Key
Alice Turner Curtis	Charles Dudley Warner	Emerson Hough
Alice Dunbar	Charles Farrar Browne	Emilie F. Carlen
Allen Chapman	Charles Ives	Emily Bronte
Alleyne Ireland	Charles Kingsley	Emily Dickinson
Ambrose Bierce	Charles Klein	Enid Bagnold
Amelia E. Barr	Charles Hanson Towne	Enilor Macartney Lane
Amory H. Bradford	Charles Lathrop Pack	Erasmus W. Jones
Andrew Lang	Charles Romyn Dake	Ernie Howard Pie
Andrew McFarland Davis	Charles Whibley	Ethel May Dell
Andy Adams	Charles Willing Beale	Ethel Turner
Angela Brazil	Charlotte M. Braeme	Ethel Watts Mumford
Anna Alice Chapin	Charlotte M. Yonge	Eugene Sue
Anna Sewell	Charlotte Perkins Stetson	Eugenie Foa
Annie Besant	Clair W. Hayes	Eugene Wood
Annie Hamilton Donnell	Clarence Day Jr.	Eustace Hale Ball
Annie Payson Call	Clarence E. Mulford	Evelyn Everett-green
Annie Roe Carr	Clemence Housman	Everard Cotes
Annonaymous	Confucius	F. H. Cheley
Anton Chekhov	Coningsby Dawson	F. J. Cross
Archibald Lee Fletcher	Cornelis DeWitt Wilcox	F. Marion Crawford
Arnold Bennett	Cyril Burleigh	Fannie E. Newberry
Arthur C. Benson	D. H. Lawrence	Federick Austin Ogg
Arthur Conan Doyle	Daniel Defoe	Ferdinand Ossendowski
Arthur M. Winfield	David Garnett	Fergus Hume
Arthur Ransome	Dinah Craik	Florence A. Kilpatrick
Arthur Schnitzler	Don Carlos Janes	Fremont B. Deering
Arthur Train	Donald Keyhoe	Francis Bacon
Atticus	Dorothy Kilner	Francis Darwin
B.H. Baden-Powell	Dougan Clark	Frances Hodgson Burnett
B. M. Bower	Douglas Fairbanks	Frances Parkinson Keyes
B. C. Chatterjee	E. Nesbit	Frank Gee Patchin
Baroness Emmuska Orczy	E. P. Roe	Frank Harris
Baroness Orczy	E. Phillips Oppenheim	Frank Jewett Mather
Basil King	E. S. Brooks	Frank L. Packard
Bayard Taylor	Earl Barnes	Frank V. Webster
Ben Macomber	Edgar Rice Burroughs	Frederic Stewart Isham
Bertha Muzzy Bower	Edith Van Dyne	Frederick Trevor Hill
Bjornstjerne Bjornson	Edith Wharton	Frederick Winslow Taylor

Friedrich Kerst
Friedrich Nietzsche
Fyodor Dostoyevsky
G.A. Henty
G.K. Chesterton
Gabrielle E. Jackson
Garrett P. Serviss
Gaston Leroux
George A. Warren
George Ade
Geroge Bernard Shaw
George Cary Eggleston
George Durston
George Ebers
George Eliot
George Gissing
George MacDonald
George Meredith
George Orwell
George Sylvester Viereck
George Tucker
George W. Cable
George Wharton James
Gertrude Atherton
Gordon Casserly
Grace E. King
Grace Gallatin
Grace Greenwood
Grant Allen
Guillermo A. Sherwell
Gulielma Zollinger
Gustav Flaubert
H. A. Cody
H. B. Irving
H.C. Bailey
H. G. Wells
H. H. Munro
H. Irving Hancock
H. R. Naylor
H. Rider Haggard
H. W. C. Davis
Haldeman Julius
Hall Caine
Hamilton Wright Mabie
Hans Christian Andersen
Harold Avery
Harold McGrath
Harriet Beecher Stowe
Harry Castlemon
Harry Coghill
Harry Houidini

Hayden Carruth
Helent Hunt Jackson
Helen Nicolay
Hendrik Conscience
Hendy David Thoreau
Henri Barbusse
Henrik Ibsen
Henry Adams
Henry Ford
Henry Frost
Henry James
Henry Jones Ford
Henry Seton Merriman
Henry W Longfellow
Herbert A. Giles
Herbert Carter
Herbert N. Casson
Herman Hesse
Hildegard G. Frey
Homer
Honore De Balzac
Horace B. Day
Horace Walpole
Horatio Alger Jr.
Howard Pyle
Howard R. Garis
Hugh Lofting
Hugh Walpole
Humphry Ward
Ian Maclaren
Inez Haynes Gillmore
Irving Bacheller
Isabel Cecilia Williams
Isabel Hornibrook
Israel Abrahams
Ivan Turgenev
J.G.Austin
J. Henri Fabre
J. M. Barrie
J. M. Walsh
J. Macdonald Oxley
J. R. Miller
J. S. Fletcher
J. S. Knowles
J. Storer Clouston
J. W. Duffield
Jack London
Jacob Abbott
James Allen
James Andrews
James Baldwin

James Branch Cabell
James DeMille
James Joyce
James Lane Allen
James Lane Allen
James Oliver Curwood
James Oppenheim
James Otis
James R. Driscoll
Jane Abbott
Jane Austen
Jane L. Stewart
Janet Aldridge
Jens Peter Jacobsen
Jerome K. Jerome
Jessie Graham Flower
John Buchan
John Burroughs
John Cournos
John F. Kennedy
John Gay
John Glasworthy
John Habberton
John Joy Bell
John Kendrick Bangs
John Milton
John Philip Sousa
John Taintor Foote
Jonas Lauritz Idemil Lie
Jonathan Swift
Joseph A. Altsheler
Joseph Carey
Joseph Conrad
Joseph E. Badger Jr
Joseph Hergesheimer
Joseph Jacobs
Jules Vernes
Julian Hawthrone
Julie A Lippmann
Justin Huntly McCarthy
Kakuzo Okakura
Karle Wilson Baker
Kate Chopin
Kenneth Grahame
Kenneth McGaffey
Kate Langley Bosher
Kate Langley Bosher
Katherine Cecil Thurston
Katherine Stokes
L. A. Abbot
L. T. Meade

L. Frank Baum
Latta Griswold
Laura Dent Crane
Laura Lee Hope
Laurence Housman
Lawrence Beasley
Leo Tolstoy
Leonid Andreyev
Lewis Carroll
Lewis Sperry Chafer
Lilian Bell
Lloyd Osbourne
Louis Hughes
Louis Joseph Vance
Louis Tracy
Louisa May Alcott
Lucy Fitch Perkins
Lucy Maud Montgomery
Luther Benson
Lydia Miller Middleton
Lyndon Orr
M. Corvus
M. H. Adams
Margaret E. Sangster
Margret Howth
Margaret Vandercook
Margaret W. Hungerford
Margret Penrose
Maria Edgeworth
Maria Thompson Daviess
Mariano Azuela
Marion Polk Angellotti
Mark Overton
Mark Twain
Mary Austin
Mary Catherine Crowley
Mary Cole
Mary Hastings Bradley
Mary Roberts Rinehart
Mary Rowlandson
M. Wollstonecraft Shelley
Maud Lindsay
Max Beerbohm
Myra Kelly
Nathaniel Hawthrone
Nicolo Machiavelli
O. F. Walton
Oscar Wilde

Owen Johnson
P.G. Wodehouse
Paul and Mabel Thorne
Paul G. Tomlinson
Paul Severing
Percy Brebner
Percy Keese Fitzhugh
Peter B. Kyne
Plato
Quincy Allen
R. Derby Holmes
R. L. Stevenson
R. S. Ball
Rabindranath Tagore
Rahul Alvares
Ralph Bonehill
Ralph Henry Barbour
Ralph Victor
Ralph Waldo Emmerson
Rene Descartes
Ray Cummings
Rex Beach
Rex E. Beach
Richard Harding Davis
Richard Jefferies
Richard Le Gallienne
Robert Barr
Robert Frost
Robert Gordon Anderson
Robert L. Drake
Robert Lansing
Robert Lynd
Robert Michael Ballantyne
Robert W. Chambers
Rosa Nouchette Carey
Rudyard Kipling
Saint Augustine
Samuel B. Allison
Samuel Hopkins Adams
Sarah Bernhardt
Sarah C. Hallowell
Selma Lagerlof
Sherwood Anderson
Sigmund Freud
Standish O'Grady
Stanley Weyman
Stella Benson
Stella M. Francis

Stephen Crane
Stewart Edward White
Stijn Streuvels
Swami Abhedananda
Swami Parmananda
T. S. Ackland
T. S. Arthur
The Princess Der Ling
Thomas A. Janvier
Thomas A Kempis
Thomas Anderton
Thomas Bailey Aldrich
Thomas Bulfinch
Thomas De Quincey
Thomas Dixon
Thomas H. Huxley
Thomas Hardy
Thomas More
Thornton W. Burgess
U. S. Grant
Upton Sinclair
Valentine Williams
Various Authors
Vaughan Kester
Victor Appleton
Victor G. Durham
Victoria Cross
Virginia Woolf
Wadsworth Camp
Walter Camp
Walter Scott
Washington Irving
Wilbur Lawton
Wilkie Collins
Willa Cather
Willard F. Baker
William Dean Howells
William le Queux
W. Makepeace Thackeray
William W. Walter
William Shakespeare
Winston Churchill
Yei Theodora Ozaki
Yogi Ramacharaka
Young E. Allison
Zane Grey